OUT
OF THE
WORMHOLE

KRISTI DOWNARD

Out of the Wormhole

ISBN: 978-1-7348873-0-3 (Print)
        978-1-7348873-1-0 (eBook)

Printed in the United States of America

Cover and Interior design: 1106 Design

THANK YOU

FIRST, I WOULD LIKE TO THANK Mary Ann Sewell. Since we met five years ago, you have been a constant beacon of friendship, encouragement, and support. Janna Vigue, you were my initial inspiration to begin writing; thank you for believing in me. Sara Mora, your help with technical issues and your superb editing skills greatly improved this book. Randall Ullom, thank you for answering my legal questions. Nakia Bailor, I loved your intricate thoughts I would never have contemplated. Thanks also to the following friends for their encouragement: Carrie Kessler, Michelle Douglas, Rosalie Fermo-Ullom, Krista Jo Smith, and Kiersta Perrson. Last but not least, I also want to thank my husband, Jimmy, for telling me to go for it.

"What a lovely surprise to finally discover
how unlonely being alone can be."

— Ellen Burstyn

PROLOGUE

MY FEET ARE ABLE TO touch the ground now. I no longer need the piece of wood to get onto the swing. The chain is rusty in some spots. My fingers get pinched sometimes, but I don't notice until I see some blood trickling down my arm. Mom is afraid I will get some sort of infection from the rusty chain, but no one gets me a new one. She just tells me to go down the slide instead. Lately, the dirt has been too dry for my skin, so the swing is my only choice. I watch my feet catch the ground as I go back and forth and back and forth. I wonder if anyone will notice.

Dad and my sister, Tammy, are playing without me, again. I hear them running through the house while Mom is making lunch. Hide-and-seek seems to be what they play the most, and I am really good at that game. They don't come to find me. Mom finds me eventually, and she will play with me.

"I know you are here!" I hear Dad yell. He sounds almost mad, so I don't know why they continue their game. I wish I could just go and play with someone else. Our closest neighbors are a ways away on each side. It takes me a long time to walk there through the woods, but when Mom is busy, I sneak off. I have a spot where I watch the other families play and make food outside. I hear them talk about school and other people and the dog. I can't get too close to either house, because the dogs might smell me, but I can still hear them talking. One family seems happier than the other one, but they both sound nice. I pretend I am part of their family in my own special game I play. My family is nice, too, but Dad looks at me sometimes and just stares. I know he hates the way I look. Then he looks away and gets up to leave. He has a hard time staying still. Tammy has all of his attention lately.

I should be glad I'm able to go outside; Mom doesn't fuss over me as much now. I think she's making grilled cheese for lunch. I am getting hungry. After lunch, I'll sneak over to the blue house and see if they've gotten the trampoline fixed yet.

Then I hear running and screaming in the house. Tammy runs outside, crying; she falls to the ground and covers her eyes.

"Oh, my God, oh, my God!" Mom yells as she runs outside too. She collapses on top of Tammy, and they cry together. I am off the swing by now and very confused about what's happening. Mom looks up to see me, and she cries even more. Tammy is wrapped up in a ball and hiding her face. Mom tells me to wait outside while she makes a phone call. She walks toward the driveway and talks to someone on her phone. I look toward the house and step inside. Very quiet. I see nothing, including Dad. I slowly walk up the stairs; I hear every creak, which seem much louder now. I edge toward Mom and Dad's room, and I look inside, just as I hear Mom coming back in and yelling my name.

"Paul, where are you?" She is still crying. Then I see Dad hanging from the light in the ceiling. He has a rope around his neck, and a chair is knocked over. I see only his backside; one shoe is off. I turn around quickly and run toward the steps as Mom is coming up. She grabs me, holds me tight, and carries me back outside. She doesn't say anything to me, because we both know why Dad did this. It's because of me.

I WAS FIVE YEARS OLD when 9/11 happened. I had only
been out of the hospital for a few months. It took some of the
focus off of me. Mom was in the kitchen, making us pancakes,
and Dad was at work. My grandmother called the house, and
my mom turned on the TV. Her crying and complete lack
of attention to my needs help me remember that day. Mom
hardly ever watched TV. She was always putting some lotion
on my skin and checking my bandages. I had to drink plenty
of fluids and couldn't do anything fun like bathtub splashing
or dirt digging, and no pets were allowed. We had to keep my
risk of infection down. After 9/11, I was not quite as big a deal.

    I didn't understand what was happening at the time, but I
liked it. I would sneak into the bathroom and play in the sink
or go outside and dig a hole in the dirt. Earthworms were my
favorite thing to play with. They had wrinkled skin, like me,
and it felt the same as mine — tough and full of ridges. Well,

the big ones were tough. The little ones were just squishy. I liked the big ones. Mom didn't like to find them in my room, all dried out, under my bed. She didn't yell, but she had that look in her eyes that made me leave the worms alone for a while. Dad didn't know anything about my fascination, and I don't remember much about him.

Now I'm twenty-two, and today is 9/11. Driving to work, I hear the announcer talk about the day of remembrance and the sacrifices this country has made for independence. I think about my first steps toward independence from the constant fussing. Living on my own now is great. I'm alone, but that's normal for me; I am alone even with people. Very few people acknowledge me in a personable way. I enjoy going to work to see those few. Now the radio guy is talking about the firefighters. No need for a hero at my job. I can be late, leave early, and sometimes not even show up, and I'll still have my job. I don't usually do any of those things, because I don't have much of a life outside of work. My boss, Brandon, is cool; he manages the restaurant. I arrive at Bayliner's Myrtle Beach Oceanfront Resort, which is on South Ocean Boulevard and right on the beach. I park close to the far south end of the resort, which is close to Papi's; I walk past the bar and through the dining room to see how busy it is. The folks might have been talking about the tragedy of the lost lives, towers falling, and the sacrifices, but when I go by, they become silent. I head to the back of the kitchen, where no one can see me. There is quite a pile of dishes waiting for me already. It's close to the end of the summer season — the last rush of vacationers. When I'm not here, it takes two people to do my job. I've been here for more than two years now and can do this job very fast. I guess I'm the hero of clean plates, cups, mugs, pitchers, platters, pots, and pans. I don't need gloves, because my fingers are already heat resistant. I do wear the nonskid shoes and protective clothing. Most people don't stay on the job long enough to tailor their outerwear to the necessary conditions.

Another bin full of dirty plates covered with food is set down on my far right. They were probably hiding that somewhere. While a load is going through the dish tank, I fill up a recently emptied rack. Glasses are the easiest, of course. So much wasted food. I use hot water while rinsing the food to keep the grease from building up in the drain. I can tell if I haven't been here for even two days. The drains are sluggish, and I have to pour some degreaser down them. Another pet peeve is coming in and finding pots left for me to scrub. Brandon says there just isn't anyone to do them. I do the dinner rush most evenings. When I walk out to the floor to put clean dishes away, it suddenly gets quiet again, and people stare. This happens most places I go.

I walk back to my steam room, and there's a stench of greasy fries. I haven't eaten French fries for months. Just cannot stand the smell. Most fried food turns my stomach; however, cheeseburgers and pizza are my main sources of nutrition. My mom wouldn't like to know that. I don't have many bad habits, except maybe the one.

I left Michigan to begin my independence, which never would've happened living at home. Mom fussed over me till the day I left. My sister, Tammy, told me I would have to move away or be a mama's boy forever. I decided on Myrtle Beach because of one thing: girls. Girls in bikinis. Girls in short shorts. Girls with no bras. Girls. What better place to live? The summer season has nearly ended, but there will still be plenty of bikini-clad girls left to look at. Now there are fewer children running around, which makes it the best time of year. My grandparents on my dad's side also live here, so that is another reason. I do like the security of family.

I do miss Mom sometimes. She has always been there for me. When I was four, I pulled a pot of chili soup onto myself from the stove. I received third-degree burns on more than half of my face, front torso, hands, and arms. I'm lucky to be alive, or so I was told. I don't remember the spill because it didn't hurt for very long, but I remember the time in the hospital. I was rushed to the University of Michigan Health Center. The burn unit was ready for me. I spent three months there. The pain started when they had to scrape off dead skin. I had multiple surgeries; several skin grafts were taken from my back. I was hooked up to several IVs, and the pictures of me look terrible. I was all swollen up and red. Now I have a frightening face. I could go around wearing a *Phantom of the Opera* mask, but I don't care anymore. My arms and hands are mostly scarred, just not as bad as my face and torso. I must have shaken them off. I'm used to being the center of attention when I walk into a room, but it's distant attention. Like I'm something they have never seen before, a surprise freak.

Before work, I sometimes hang out at my personal shaded spot with my Michigan ball cap and sunglasses on. My tree is perfectly situated, away from the outside bar, with a great view of the beach and bodies to look at. Girls. I wonder what their smooth skin feels like. They look so much softer than men. What do they smell like? What would their hair feel like against my skin? Girls are such a mystery. I do work with some girls. Taylor is close to my age. She has long, red, curly hair. Her face is full of freckles, and her skin is so tan. She smells like coconuts and lime most of the time. Once, she smelled like honey, but just the once. Sometimes she puts one side of her hair in a clip or something, and the other side is down. The waitresses can wear any kind of shirt and slacks. They just have to wear a red apron over whatever they're wearing. We work in a burger-joint restaurant just off the beach, inside the far end of the resort. There is a bar just outside the doors with patio tables. The outside is shaded with interweaving canvases that sway in the breeze. It is a nice resort to work at and to enjoy the scenery. There is a much fancier restaurant inside, which I applied for. Administration thought I would be better suited for the burger joint. I would get paid more inside at "The Flamingo," but they weren't hiring at that time. I guess they still aren't. That's okay. I would miss seeing Taylor if I left. She's nice to me and smiles all the time. She comes out to sit by me under my tree if we are slow. I make sure to be sitting where the breeze is blowing her scent my way.

I also work with Beth. She's different from Taylor. Her hair is long and black. I don't think her hair is naturally that black, but it does look like silk. I picture my white fingers running through it. She's nice to me, but she's mad at men most of the time. I'm sure she wouldn't hesitate to punch me if I touched her hair. She smells like flowers most days. I like that too. Beth is a little older than Taylor and me. The three of us are the only single people I talk to who work here. Brandon just got married, and Joe is recently divorced. Joe is the outside bartender. They are the only friends I have. There are other workers, but they don't talk to me much. I used to have friends in the chat rooms when I'd play "Destiny" and "Minecraft," but I've gotten away from that. When winter gets here, I'll have to reconnect with them when there are no girls to look at.

Taylor is my favorite, though. She works most days and is saving her money to buy an Airstream camper. She wants to travel the countryside, selling western wear out of it at events. She also works in housekeeping to pick up more hours, because she gets tired doing the same job. She tells me stories of things she has found while cleaning the rooms. Most of the time, she talks about sex toys or used condoms. I'm fascinated by her stories. Sounds so crazy, but she's probably exaggerating to make me laugh. Taylor doesn't know she is my best friend.

My shift is nearly done, and I'm one of the last ones to leave. Beth is the late waitress tonight. Her hair is in a ponytail. While I'm putting away the last of the glasses, she quickly passes by me for a pitcher, and her hair runs over my right arm. The sense of feeling is sharper in my upper arms than in my hands. It tickles a little and smells so good. Beth will give me a few dollars some nights when her tips are good. Tonight is not one of those nights. She pops back to tell me she's leaving; I usually lock up. Still thinking about her hair on my arms. I know what I'll be doing tonight.

As I leave, I see couples kissing on the beach or in the parking lot. Their hands are all over each other. They don't even notice the freak close to them. I get into my car and drive home. I live in Toddville, which is about a twenty-minute drive from Bayliner's. I drive through the Waccamaw National Wildlife Refuge to the Waccamaw Bend mobile home park. Nothing fancy, but it's all mine. My trailer is the last one in a line. My grandfather found it for sale and told me about it. The previous owner died. Great location with some shade trees, and no trailers on one side. My one neighbor is an old lady; she keeps to herself. I have a peaceful view of the vast prairie, with several eagle sightings. I also hear woodpeckers. It took a while to get used to their hammering; I don't even hear it now. I've been told there are alligators in the wetlands, but I haven't seen any. I stopped walking on the trail to Halfway Swamp when I heard that.

I already ate dinner at the restaurant, so I can get right to my bad habit. My adult-film library is kept hidden inside a shoe box. I'm afraid to look up porn online — too many viruses. I find the disk labeled *Lust After Alicia*. This girl reminds me of Beth, and after feeling Beth's hair, this won't take long. I have my emu lotion and tissues. Emu lotion is what I put on my scars every day. Once a day is plenty, now that I work in such a humid environment. Alicia is such a bad girl. I try to picture what sex would be like in real life — full of warm, squishy breasts, round, full ass, actual eye contact, and sex to name a few things. Girls are mythical. I'm stuck with my imagination to do the rest. My only problem is that porn is so fake. The acting is bad. The storyline is always the same: girl can't pay bill, girl can't fix her car, or it's her first time. Sometimes I just turn the volume down and make up the stories and sounds in my mind. What would they really be saying? Or what would it smell like getting all sweaty? I've lost many of my sweat glands, but my nose works fine, what's left of it.

I try to picture what it would really be like; I put myself there. Isn't that what all guys do? Especially ones who have never gotten to have sex? I'm twenty-two and screwed forever. I'm a porn addict who hates watching it. I want my *own* story of love and sex. I see beautiful people all day. Then I catch myself in a reflection on the vast amount of stainless steel at work or in the bathroom mirror. Horror picture. One eye is barely a hole to look out of. The left side of my face looks like I'm melting. My mouth can't open fully. My nose is mostly gone. I have one good eye, and only half my hair is there, on my right side. When I cover up the rest with a blanket and can only see the top-right part of my face, I'm not bad looking. *Paul, you look dashing today. Paul, can you come and sit with us? Paul, let me take my clothes off for you.*

I have thought about a hooker just to get it over with. I think I'll be trying that soon. At least I would be able to touch, smell, and really experience what that hole feels like. I want some sort of emotional connection. I want panting and grinding. My penis is the one thing unaffected by the chili. Some days the sink drain hole even looks inviting. "Obsessed" is putting it lightly. If there was a support group for ugly guys who have not been laid, I would be president.

2

I'M OFF WORK TODAY, so I decide to visit Ed and Jean Duram, my grandparents. They live close to me. They have a shop on Flagg Street called "Hooks." When you walk into the store, it's outrageous. The fish smell is partly masked with plug-in cinnamon air fresheners everywhere. Very strong smell, but the visual effect is even more powerful. Fish are all over the ceiling and walls, almost like there is imaginary water filling the store. Sharks getting ready to catch the poor little fish. Swordfish spearing a small tuna. Stingray hiding beside a rock, with a puffer fish perched on it. In the corner is an octopus with its tentacles actually holding a sword, ready to attack. That one is not for sale and very dusty. My grandfather likes to pose the fish in attack positions and sell them to restaurants. Most of the fish are sold to him from fishermen. They were either killed in a net, or the meat was sold, and they sell him the hide. The rest of his business is from customers bringing

OUT OF THE WORMHOLE

in freshly caught fish to put up on their wall. He just displays them on a board, sometimes with some fake seaweed around them. I would have loved to work here, but, unfortunately, the instruments he uses are small, and my hands have a hard time holding on and doing the detailed work. Destroyed nerves.

Grandma is taking care of a customer who brought in a small reef shark. They decide on a simple display, and she tells them to come back in three days. I walk on back to see Grandpa. He wants to give me a hug, but he has just finished cutting out the insides of a sheepshead porgy. He's filling in the eyes and inside of the head cavity with his white putty paste. This fish isn't very big; it's the size of a dinner plate. He will have it stuffed and the fins pinned out to dry within two hours and will shoot some paint on it tomorrow. He makes the fish look even better dead.

"What're you up to today?" Ed says.

"Did you sell that tortoise you were working on last week?" I ask.

"I did, and I never want to do another one. The skin was so tough. Sounds like I have another shark to do." He smiles at that. Grandpa likes to do sharks. They are the easiest. Not so much fin work or ligaments to cut. The paint jobs are also faster and easier. He doesn't have to fill in all the individual scales. He still charges top rate for them, though, because they are easier. They make a good living with Hooks. He has a thirty-five-pound cut-off in size now. Too much for him to handle. Grandma comes back with the poor dead shark and throws it in the fridge.

"Are ya staying for dinner tonight?" she asks.

"No, I can't take the smell in here for that long." I smile while she looks at me, rolling her eyes.

"We can go out to your favorite spot tonight, followed by ice cream at Nathan's." Grandpa knows how I like their hot dogs and ice cream. I don't want to say I'm too old to hang around with them, but I am; sometimes I feel obligated. Nathan's is one of the places I go to regularly, and the staff is used to me. I keep to the same stores and restaurants. Not so much staring.

"I'm just going to go hang out by Papi's. Taylor said she may stop by and hang after she gets done cleaning her rooms."

"Do you like Taylor?" Grandma asks. She worries that I've never had a girlfriend. What does she expect? Family sees past the freak, but the rest of the world does not.

"We're getting married next week," I tell her with a straight face.

"We'll stuff a big dolphin for you to hang in your trailer for your wedding present," Grandpa chuckles.

"I was really hoping for a stingray with a big butcher knife in its mouth ... please?" I egg him on. He laughs.

"Good idea, kid." Another customer comes in. I clean up the fish guts and mop the floor for Grandpa before I leave. Then I wave goodbye while that customer holds a small shark they want mounted for their grandson.

Myrtle Beach is a fun place to live: dinosaur parks, the sky wheel, car shows, and weddings all the time. But the girls are all I'm interested in.

I park my Elantra at work and get my comfy chair out of the trunk. I walk around to the end of the resort and happily find my favorite tree unoccupied. I get comfy in the shade.

Direct sun is too much for my skin. I can tell that it's slow at Papi's; the dinner rush hasn't come in from the beach. It's my day off, and, once again, I'm at work. People-watching takes skill. Under my hat and sunglasses, am I reading, or staring at you, or asleep? Nobody knows.

I see a couple in the water with their arms around each other, kissing. That isn't fake, and no cameras are going to zoom in on the couple paid to act like they are having a good time. The waves push her over one last time while they are getting out. He helps her up. When they reach their towels, he rolls on top of her, and they kiss some more. I look around for other people watching them. Just me. Does she taste salty now? Probably still tastes good. Her hair is all stuck to both their heads like an alien. What do men and women even talk about? There can't be that much in common. Soon they gather their belongings and head into Bayliner's. I wonder if they just got married, or maybe they're celebrating an anniversary. They will shower and clean up to get ready to go out to dinner later on. They might even eat at The Flamingo, a place where only pretty people work to serve other pretty people.

"What're you staring at?" Taylor asks me as she brings a chair over from the outside tables. She's brought us both a drink in cupholders while dragging a chair.

"I'm sorry. I would have helped. I was looking at the waves and thinking about something. I don't even remember." Taylor arranges her chair in the sand. Her hair is in a puffy bun on top of her head. She smells more like cleaners now and is wearing her maid's uniform. It's a light-green, scrub-type dress with white shoes. She has her keys hanging around her neck on a bright-pink lanyard. It holds membership cards to several stores, and I see her universal card for getting into the rooms to clean them. Not many actual keys. She's drinking a peach margarita, and I'm having the usual Tom Collins.

"Have you been out here all day?" she asks.

"No, I went to see Ed and Jean and helped them out." Taylor has met my grandparents. They were so thrilled to see me with someone that day. Taylor still talks about the crazy fish place. She was the first person, other than family, ever to ride in a car with me. I was so nervous trying to drive with a girl in my car. I wanted to put down the windows and drive real slow so the world could see me. I'm not alone today! She may just feel sorry for me, and if that's the case, I don't even want to know.

"Anything crazy cleaning rooms today?" I ask.

"Oh, yes — the usual hazards on the floor. One room had a big black dildo just sitting right on the table. It was so gross. I threw a towel over it to clean the room, or it would've looked at me the whole time." We both laugh while she's telling the story. Always sounds crazy.

"Another room had five half-eaten pizzas under the bed still in boxes, which I would not have even seen except for the smell. There was a bit of pot smell too; they were hungry." I picture all of the pizza under the bed trying to hide from being eaten. I'll be sad when she makes enough money to quit working here and hits the road. We sit in silence for a while; she just keeps drinking and looking at the water. Her lips are dry. She needs some ChapStick® or something on them. I wish I could put it on her. Her lips are plump, while mine are nonexistent.

"Can I ask you something?" I say.

"Sure, ask away," she replies.

"Why do you talk to me? It's okay to be honest. I've heard it all. I can take it."

She hesitates.

"Paul, everyone needs friends, and I always see you alone. I had a friend in elementary school who had a small burn on her arm, and the other kids were so mean to her just for that. You must've been bullied so much. You are not all macho and stupid, either. I have fun talking to you."

"Thanks." I thought about what she said. "I wasn't bullied as much as you probably think. My mom kept me at home all through school. I went to church and sang in the choir. That was one of the few times I went anywhere. Those people there were used to me; so I was not such a big deal. Some of the kids at church were mean, of course. Then I moved here. It hasn't been too bad." We stare at the few people left on the beach. A large cruise ship is far in the distance. So many couples are on that ship, having a great time together in their private lives.

"Glad to hear it. Are you going to stay here for a long time?"

"I like it here. Where else would I go?" I answer.

"Hey, I have to get ready for work again. Enjoy your day off, loser." She takes the chair back. I think about the kissing couple on the beach again. I wonder if my prediction was right. I decide to test it out. At about 6:30 p.m., I put my chair back in my car and hang out in the lobby for a bit, standing behind a rack like I'm looking at the postcards. I watch the people coming off the elevators. Couple. Couple.

Group. Couple. Then I see them. She has on a yellow dress with the little straps. The bottom is all choppy and sways around with her movement. I wonder if they had sex again upstairs. I wish I could be a fly on that wall. They go into The Flamingo — just as I thought. They sit in a faraway private corner; must be newlyweds. They can't keep their hands off each other. He's telling her how hot she looks and how much he just wants to skip dinner and go back upstairs. She's telling him that she's hungry and that he'll have to wait a little longer. He growls in her ear like a bear and slips his hand up her dress. Her head flies back, and she yells for more. I snap out of my trance; maybe that's just in the videos.

I find a quiet spot in a lobby chair and hide behind a magazine where I can see people coming and going. Here comes the yellow dress. Her long, blond hair must smell like peaches. No, I bet it smells like apples. They head for the elevators. I get up and get on the same elevator. I keep my back to them. They are giggling behind me. Usually when I'm on an elevator, everyone gets real quiet. They are so entranced with each other; they don't even notice another passenger. On the sixth floor, they walk around me. I stay on till the last moment, and then I quietly step off. What am I doing? Listening to their conversations, seeing how they interact, and I do smell something fruity. I watch as they laugh and play down the hallway. When they are halfway down, I start walking, with my head lowered. They reach their room, and he inserts the key card. Just before the door closes, I hear her scream in delight. I stand close to their door and listen. It's quiet. Their mouths are busy. Then I hear her say something.

"Hurry, hurry, Babe — put it on." More giggling. I walk away before someone catches me standing there. I picture the intense sex they are having. Doesn't that hurt her? He is a big guy. How does that work? The guys are fairly average-sized and tame in the videos I see. Easygoing. Girl is on top a lot, so her boobs can bounce around. How does a girl have an orgasm? I have heard that girls smell like fish. I can't imagine that's true, after the fish I cleaned up today. What does that really mean? So many questions. Is my reality clouded from the fake videos? Will I ever find out what girls actually feel like before I die?

I head back downstairs and walk toward the hallway that leads to Papi's. I sit at the outside bar with another Tom Collins. Joe is the usual bartender outside. He never charges me for my drinks. I think he works here just to see the bikinis too. Neither of us have anyplace better to be. I need to find a different pastime. A hobby. What can a man who looks like me even do? Boring future of watching beachgoers from afar.

I think about my mom. Is she glad I'm out of the house? She will date and come and go without worrying about leaving me home or taking me with her. She has dated a few different men. I liked them all okay. She doesn't want a serious relationship, though. Her name is Phyllis. After my father committed suicide, she decided to go back to school. I was eight by then. Mom went to nursing school. She said she admired the nurses who took care of me in the burn unit day after day. That's what she does now. She's sympathetic to all their needs, having gone through it herself. She lives in Brighton, Michigan. She has always lived there. It's a very cute little town with the naked-irregular-man statue in front of Mill Pond. I've always felt like he was there for me, somehow; his outer skin is irregular and crumpled. Kids sometimes dress him up for the holidays. I haven't been back to Brighton since I left two years ago. Mom has come down twice.

My glass is empty. A fly lands on my hand. I don't even notice it till I look down and see a black spot. A fly on the wall. How could I be a fly on the wall? Maybe I should just head back to the trailer.

"Pizza burger to go, Joe!"

3

I LEFT MY MOM A voicemail this morning. She's no doubt at work. She likes me to check in with her to let her know I'm doing fine. I wonder if Mom makes my sister check in. My sister, Tammy, is five years older. She lives in Howell, Michigan, not far from Brighton. My sister doesn't get too close to people in general. She keeps a very low profile — like almost invisible. She works full-time in an antique shop, which suits her personality, which is standoffish. I'm sure this all stems from the attention I received growing up. It made her an outcast. My sister had a daughter when she was very young, my niece, Jamie. That's probably my fault, also: neglected daughter craves love from the outside. When school is over for my niece, the bus drops her off at the store, where she has a hidden cubby behind the furniture that's all hers to read and draw in. Jamie is eleven now, I think. Her dad is Johnny Larabee. He has Jamie every other weekend. Johnny is a nice guy. They never wanted to get married. Johnny works at the Ford plant in Detroit. I don't know if they are dating each other now or other people. I gave up keeping track after I moved away. My sister and I don't talk much. I miss seeing them, but I like having my own space and independence.

My mom's parents, Tom and Sandy, live on Mackinac Island during tourist season. They dress up in vintage-like clothes and work at a fudge shop. I enjoyed riding on the bike trail around the island. I would cover up my skin, and the breeze off the lake was cool. I would do more biking now, but it's too hot here most of the time, and my skin would be exposed to the sun and then to people's stares. I'll just stick with the shade trees and girl-watching. When tourist season is over, Tom and Sandy head for The Keys. They keep a camper in the same place year round. Both sets of my grandparents are very fun and unique. Tammy, Jamie, and Mom go to Mackinac several times a year to see them. I wonder if they're glad I wasn't with them this summer, because they wouldn't have onlookers staring and pointing. They won't have to worry about my needs or feelings. It must be a relief for them. The freak is gone!

Mom can put mirrors up in the bathroom now. While growing up, the only mirror in the house was in Mom's room. She would use it for her makeup, and then would fold it up. I hardly ever saw myself. I have a mirror in my bathroom now. The man looking back at me is usually frustrated with himself or just checking to see if the lotion is all rubbed in. On two rare occasions, I have seen someone who looks like me, all scarred up from burns. We stare at each other with knowing eyes, like looking into a mirror. We feel the anguish through each other — our tortured lives. We don't go up and hug or shake hands. It's a code of acknowledgment, the perception of our reality. No words need to be said. Maybe we are heroes in the respect that we have to live this way.

I hear a loud banging on my trailer door. Very unusual to have a visitor. When I open the door, there is a small boy who looks at me and screams, and then he runs away. Down the road, he's met by his little buddies, and they run away laughing. Glad I can make them laugh, but I really should check who it is first. I could buy a normal face mask and scare them back next time. I see my neighbor, Bonnie, in the window. She seems lonely, and I never see anyone visiting her. Bonnie is probably around seventy, I would guess. She's very overweight and has her food delivered sometimes. The woodpeckers are busy this morning, so I close the door and decide to watch some porn before going to work. Daylight porn doesn't seem as perverse as night porn.

Arriving at work at 3:00 p.m. will give me time to clean up the leftover mess before I start the new mess. Slow drains and food on the floor. Paul will get it tonight — no worries. The shift goes fast because it's Friday night. Taylor gives me a little of her tip money. I wish Taylor and I could be more than just friends, but I know she doesn't feel that way about me. Should I get her a friendship gift? What is the protocol here? I see her purse and neck strap full of her keys hanging on the hook right outside of the kitchen, close to my station. Maybe I could get her a trinket to hang on her ... then I see the room key that allows her access to all the rooms. My mind tells me to go — go and get it. Why? I look down the hall and into the kitchen. Everybody is busy, and no one is close to me. I immediately go to her keys. The resort key card looks worn, like it could easily break off. My fingers have to work hard at starting the plastic key under the hook ring, but I get it. Round and round the loop, and it's off; it's in my hands. Right into my back pocket, and I'm back to my stack of dirty plates.

My mind is swirling with what I've just done. Before I could even talk myself out of it, I was taking it. Why did I do that? I think that was my first crime. My legs are feeling a little weak. I can't concentrate. Needing some air, I go out the back door, stumble behind the dumpsters, and sit down in the sand. I close my eyes and listen to the distant waves. Why? Quit fooling yourself, Paul. You *know* why. You are fascinated with what goes on behind closed doors: the communication, the togetherness, and the sex. You love Taylor's stories about what she finds in the rooms. You want to see it for yourself. I feel for the plastic key in my back pocket, and it really is there. Then I hear the familiar giggling in the parking lot. It's that couple; they are still here. I peek around again to see their fierce kissing up against their car. It's after 8:00 p.m. now, so they already had dinner. Probably some drinks, and then they will go back to the room for crazy-sex time. Stop thinking, Paul. You can't be a part of their lives. You are a freak who will have to live alone, and you need to accept it. But now I'm a criminal, because I crossed that line. I could live in solitude in jail the same as I do now, right?

I go back in and find Brandon looking for me.

"I had to get some air; I don't feel so good." I rub my stomach. Brandon knows I hardly ever miss work. I can see the disappointment in his eyes, but he tells me to go home. I walk by the hooks and see Taylor's keys still hanging there, looking undisturbed. I wonder when she will realize something is missing, and I hope she doesn't get into trouble. I sit in my car for a few minutes. There's nowhere I have to go, no one to see, and there's no one who cares where I am tonight. I could go to my empty trailer and watch my perverted repetitive crap, or I could do something else entirely. Something that would give me a thrill like nothing else in my life has ever come close to.

My mind cannot deny my thoughts. I get out of my car and walk toward the back door, swipe in, take the steps up to the sixth floor, and stand outside their room, 633. My breathing needs to calm down from the climb. The room is quiet, the same as the hall. The couple is not here yet. My heart is pounding. I get out the key from my back pocket and easily open the door. It's dark and empty, as expected. There's an array of scents I notice first, flowery mixed with suntan lotion. I go to the bathroom, turn on the light, and look at her girly things: lipstick, lip gloss, ChapStick, hair bands, and a brush. I pick up the brush and smell it; not much aroma, but it has sticky stuff on the bristles, and yet it's still wonderful. I get excited just touching something so personal. I put everything back after I smell it. I walk into the bedroom. The bed is messy. I do see a condom on the floor. I look closely at it. The smell around the bed is familiar, yet also mixed with perfume. Then, for some reason, I look under the bed. It's not a solid piece. There is a covering that hangs to the floor and the floor looks somewhat clean under the bed, with no pizza boxes. No crazy black dildos or dirty clothes. The clothes I'm wearing are quiet. *What are you thinking, Paul?* Need to urinate. I pee and flip the light back off.

I slide under the bed and fold the edging back down just so. There's about an inch between me and the metal wire under the box spring. My body fits easily at five feet eight and around 150 pounds. I decide to lie along the wall at the top of the bed, hopefully less hazardous to me. Are you really going to do this? How would they ever know I was even here? I'm not sick; I won't be coughing. My bladder can go for hours if necessary. Here's my chance to be a fly on the wall and experience real-life communication and real-life sex. I can't believe I'm under here; now, I just have to wait. My heart is beating hard and fast; they'll hear my heart first. *Paul, what are you doing?* I think about the consequences. Are you really going to stay under this bed with these strangers? I start to panic and think *I'd better get out of here. What would your family think if you got caught?*

That's it. I start to scoot out when I hear someone outside the door. I scoot back under and fix the edging again. I hear the little beep, and the door opens. I'm in for the show now. Slow your breathing down; relax. Just enjoy the show in your mind. Close your eyes. Nobody will know. You deserve to experience real-life people situations.

"Did you see that lady lookin' at us like we're total trash? What a hag. I gotta pee." She's clearly drunk and slurring her words. He throws himself on the bed and I hear him yawn. Then he gets up, and it sounds like he's taking off his clothes. He walks to the bathroom.

"No more sand in the bed. Let's rinse off our feet. It smells like French fries in here."

"It does, babeeeeee … I'll get in with you." They smell me, the grease. I could probably get out of here while they are in the shower if I wanted to, but I don't really want to. I doubt they'll look under the bed for fries. The shower soon turns off. He belches. They must be drying off. She giggles again. They come back toward the bed.

"I'm soooo sad this is our last night here," she whines.

"We can't fool them much longer. In a few months, we'll make up another conference. I'll get a divorce attorney after her father's settlement goes through. Until then, we'll just have to remember this week." They are kissing now; I hear lips smacking and moaning.

"I want this to be us all the time; I can't wait." She sounds pouty. This sounds like my movie called *On the Side*, which is about cheaters getting it on. Now I don't care as much about getting caught; they won't want to get caught, either. They must be kissing more, and I hear a wrapper opening. The bed then crashes down in the middle with a rhythmic motion.

Now she is moaning and moaning and moaning. Yes, it does sound similar, funny. I'm not picking up any sweaty smells, just some more perfume. Very glad I'm up against the wall, or I would have been crushed and found out by now. I suddenly think of my cell phone. I didn't turn it off. There is a good chance no one will call or text me, since that's rare anyway, but now I'm immediately sickened. I don't think I can turn it off without a sound, but I think I can turn it way down. I reach for it out of my back pocket and turn my head.

Nice and slow, so as not to bump the bed; however, I doubt they would notice. I turn the volume down all the way. *Okay, much better now — calm down.* I slip it back into my pants, easy. I tell myself to relax all my muscles; I picture myself relaxing and breathing; everything is fine. This is what you wanted: a real live show.

They must be changing positions now. They are both moaning, and the bed is going crazy. Not sure who is on who. This does sound more real than my movies, more animal-like and more yelling now from her. Sometimes she sounds like she is in pain, then it changes to pleasure. I can tell when he blows it; he makes a long "Ahhhhhhhhh" sound. Now the bed is quiet, with just some heavy panting noises.

He gets up to go to the restroom. I know this because he jars the floor, almost shaking it. I want to lift the curtain hiding me and smell the room. What does a room smell like right after sex-burning friction, sweat, feet, cum? I stay frozen. Will another condom be on the floor?

She speaks. "I'm getting hungry again. Can we get some food?" That would be perfect if they left.

"Let's just get some room service. Call for a snack plate and wine. I don't want to get dressed again; we aren't done." His voice is very manly, like a bear.

"That sounds perfect," she answers. I wonder what I have gotten myself into here. I hear the girl call for the food, and she must be just lying on the bed. The toilet flushes, and he stomps back out. He gets on the bed. More sloppy kissing sounds, and then she is up to the restroom. The bathroom door shuts. She wants privacy. Then I hear him with his cell phone. He listens to a message. It's from a female, but I can't make it out — his wife, perhaps, wondering how his conference is going. I would say it's going well and sales are up. He lays the phone back down. The toilet flushes again. She comes out and gets back onto the bed. The TV flips on.

I lie here on the floor, listening to what sounds like a *Friends* episode on TV. I hear that guy's voice making jokes about someone's hair. Mom and Dad would watch that show. Now I feel like a disgrace hiding here. I think about some memories I have left of my father. Dad had a hard time being with me after the burn. He was scared to touch me, love me, or talk to me. I know that's why he killed himself. He couldn't bear to live every day with me for a son. His parents told me he had problems with depression even before I came along. Mom said he loved me very much, but I don't remember love. I remember the look. The sadness in his eyes, the fear of my presence. *And, look where I am today, Dad — sneaking into other people's lives. If you can see me now, I'm sorry. This isn't normally me, but my life needs some involvement. I want to know about the mysteries of man and woman. People don't act normal around me; I scare them. Remember, Dad, when you seemed scared? When I had all of those surgeries to slit my scars to allow for growth? You could not even look at me. Look at me now!*

The food arrives, with a knock on the door. He gets up and walks to the door. When did he put clothes on? No idea. The cork is popped.

"To our last night together, my love," he says, toasting with a clink of the glasses.

"This makes me so sad. I hope the settlement comes through soon," she blubbers. The crunching of crackers and giggling begins again. She goes from sad to happy quickly. The TV is changed to some detective show talking about the victim being the brother of the judge. I wonder if he is lying to her about some settlement, and he's just dragging her along. That's what he sounds like to me. No other details about it. Just the "settlement."

"I've got an appointment with my attorney next month, babe. Then I'll serve the papers." She claps.

"She'll try to take everything from you — you know that, right?"

"I have most of it hidden from her. Susan will think she's getting a good deal. I started planning this the day we met." *He sure knows what to say. This would be a good movie plot.*

One of the glasses lands on the floor close to my head. *Crap, they are going to lean down and see me or sense my presence. Oh, okay — they're having sex again.*

"Oh, babeee, you're the best." She wants him bad. She moans and pants with urgency. Then the bed is rocking again. No condom this time? They grunt like some wild animals. I hope this bed is strong. I lift the edge of my curtain so I can get a better sense of the urgency. I could almost reach my hand around and feel them, but I just stare at the empty glass. It's like a crazy dream, but this is real. I feel like I'm experiencing it with them in a way. My own body gyrating ever so slightly, and this time I get a hard-on — it almost comes out of my pants. If I had my hand on it, I would have exploded with them. He lasts a long time. Feels like an hour of constant sex;

I had no idea it ever took that long. Then she gasps and yells for Brian. He gives her his famous, "Ahhhhhhhhhhhh." I can smell the sweat and sperm this time. My God, forbidden love is powerful! That was intense, and now a little scary, because I'm still here. I still need to get out.

They are watching TV again and eating. She's probably rubbing him somewhere. Another hour or so goes by. I hear her go to the restroom and get into the shower. *Please go in with her.* But he doesn't. He's on his phone again. I hear him text. I hear him laugh to himself. Then quiet. She comes out.

"My turn. Keep the bed warm for me," he mentions in passing — and then a spank. She's on her phone now. I hear her texting. I wonder if she's looking at his phone, or if he has a lock on it? I'll never know what happens with this lying, cheating couple, but I will not soon forget them. Soon he returns, and they're both eating and drinking some more. Must be sharing a glass. Now I wonder if he did put a condom on or not. They don't even talk about it if he didn't. Crazy people drama.

Later on, the room becomes silent. I can faintly hear him snoring. Is she asleep? I wait for a while longer. No movement. It's quiet and still. Must be after midnight by now. Hopefully, the wine has taken effect. I wait for another fifteen minutes or so, with just the occasional turning. I decide it's time to get out. I quietly wiggle myself out from underneath. I slowly sit up and look at them. They both look asleep. Her hair is a hot mess. They are barely covered with a sheet. Focus on getting out of here; the fly needs to go. I check my pockets for my phone and keys — check — and slowly walk to the door. I glance back. Nothing. Opening the door might wake one of them, but

I will be gone by the time they would know what happened. They didn't even turn the deadbolt. I listen for people in the hallway. Quiet. Then I open the door and close it quickly. I walk to the end of the hallway and enter the stairwell.

That's when I feel like I can actually breathe. I inhale and exhale like I was just born. I gasp and hold my stomach and laugh and cry a little. That was more real than anything else I had ever experienced. It was not even hard to get away with. Oh, yeah. I feel for the room key; it's there in my back pocket. I spend some time just breathing and reliving my experience. I ease down six glorious flights of stairs and don't remember doing it. Still on my high, I decide to go home before someone sees me. I must look crazed, if a shocked expression is even possible for my face. I don't even know.

I LINGER A LITTLE LONGER in bed this morning. Thinking
about last night, my visions scatter. The perfect bodies,
smooth skin, strong scents, and grunts of pleasure were real.
People do act that way for real. It's probably comparable to
watching porn, but the dialogue was real life. The intensity is
so different when you are in it. I felt like I was involved, there,
an active part. It has changed me, but not in a bad way. It was
rejuvenating; I'm born again. I laugh to myself for getting away
with it. I feel like I have a bond with them while I'm getting
up to use the toilet: the familiar flush, the return jump into
the bed, the snuggling in, and the bonding. The wineglass on
the floor could have been devastating, but it was like the glass
was telling me it knew I was there and kept me company. My
little friend; a drink for the fly.

I return to the bathroom and look at my face in the mirror.
This isn't the face I picture making love. When I make love

for the first time, I want to have my face covered like Zorro. I could seduce someone and stay hidden behind the mask. She will fall into my arms after I save her from the robbery in her flower store, like Spider-Man or Ant-Man. Looking at my face, it has changed some. My inner soul is now alive with risk and danger, which has left a smirk of satisfaction.

I want to talk with someone — Mom, Tammy, or Grandpa Tom, but this would not go over well with anybody, and they would know something has changed just from the sound of my voice. This little secret adventure will need to stay private. What a shame; it's the greatest thing I've ever done. To fill the rest of the day before I go to work, I watch some more movies. Such a disappointment now with the scripted dialogue, fake flattery, and their smooth, easygoing ways. No food, toilets, dropped glasses, or real-life situations like actual affairs. I'm so charged up. Perhaps there is a dating site for burn victims. Let's look … nope … nothing for the disabled, either. What a disappointment. I should start one. Maybe tomorrow.

When I arrive at work, Beth is at the counter.

"Hi, Paul. What's up?"

"Nothin.' How's the latest man quest going?"

"So far, so good. He has pissed me off only a couple times — a big improvement over the last one." She follows me all the way into my dishwashing station.

"Why are you smiling?" I didn't realize I was. "Most people don't smile coming to work, only leaving work."

"No reason," I reply. I tie my waterproof apron on. I look at the drain situation. My trash needs emptying already. She's still watching me. I turn around and look at her. "What!" I throw my arms up.

"Sorry," Beth shrugs and turns around to leave. Wish I could tell her that I'm in love or I'm seeing someone, but that doesn't happen to freaks. The dirty dishes start showing up.

During break, I take a walk outside and sit by my tree. It's still warm out in the evenings. Lots of people by the beach, strolling by, holding hands, and laughing. Mostly couples, but not my couple. They are gone, he to his wife, and she all alone, I assume. They'll get caught someday, or he will tire of her nagging him to leave his wife. I wonder if he has kids — so sad. He must have a separate cell phone to contact her; it all must be exhausting. Why do I hope they get caught? I should have stolen his phone and contacted his wife. That would have really been *involvement*. They would forever wonder how she found out. Break time is over.

Later that night, I order myself a pizza hamburger. Chef Ryan makes it especially for me. I have to chop it up on a plate because my mouth won't open that big, but it's the best of both worlds. I sit outside at the bar to eat it. I have put on more than ten pounds since moving here. *I'd better watch my weight, or I'll need another surgery of slits to allow for my belly to grow.* There is a young couple a few seats down from me. It sounds like they've just met each other. She has girlfriends close by but far enough away to give them some space. He tells her he has been to Chicago several times. Loves it there. She tells him she has never been to Indiana. More giggling, always the giggling. He's here with some buddies. They travel around setting up for bands. She's here for a bachelorette weekend. So easy for pretty people to meet and talk. If I walked over and tried to talk to them, everyone would scatter. Joe is the bartender tonight, like always, and he is chattin' it up with the girlfriends. I'll just eat my burger in peace over in my corner world. The man tells her that "Eva" is the *perfect* name for her. Her skin is perfectly bronzed, and her blond hair cascades down her shoulders. She looks just like a girl I know already, but way better in person.

When I finish eating, I carry my plate back to my sink and throw it in. I look down at my arms and feel my face. Trapped. The high I had earlier is disappearing.

The next day, I'm off work again. I ask my grandparents, Ed and Jean, if they can close up shop for lunch and meet me at Nathan's for hot dogs and ice cream. They can, so we will meet at 12:30 p.m. I need more real-life with people; I don't want to be alone. We sit outside, otherwise grandpa would stink up the restaurant with fish smell. He tells me he was mounting a swordfish this morning. He has done more of them than anything else. They talk about some of the customers' reactions to his octopus display and about their doctor visits and something about blood pressure. I act like I'm listening, but I'm just thinking about what that couple is doing now. Is he home with his wife acting like everything is fine and kissing her with those same lips? Is she crying in her pillow? I want to tell her to move on, quit being a doormat for him to use. It's so easy for me to see this in other people, because I listen. That's right, I am listening. I'm part of the conversation, and I'm thinking about other people. I'm contemplating other people's lives. It's not all about me this time; what a different concept to have. My grandparents are still talking. Perhaps I should listen to them instead. *Yes, Paul, take an interest in their lives.* In the last two years, they have seen me more than anybody. They are trying to share with me, and I'm not even listening.

Grandma goes and gets the ice cream; she knows what to get. My favorite ice cream is moose tracks. They both get butter pecan. We remain sitting under an umbrella, and there are kids close to us. They stare at me the whole time. The mother tries to get them to stop, but they don't. Once when I was around ten, I walked right up to a family like this and asked if the kids wanted to touch it. All of the kids got up and walked away, but one little boy just stared at me. He reached right out to feel my arm real slow. He looked at all of my skin and then touched my face. He asked me if it hurt and how old I was. I wish I would have gotten his name or phone number. Maybe we would be friends now. That was the only time someone other than Mom really touched me.

"Paul, I said how's work going?" Grandpa waves his hand in front of me. I'm thinking about me again.

"Oh, fine. It'll start getting real slow soon. I may have to find a second job to pay for the trailer."

"Do ya have any ideas?"

"No, but I'll figure it out." I just have to find a job that doesn't involve fine motor skills or contact with people — no problem. We finish our ice cream and part ways. The family watches me walk away. Sometimes I wave, but I'm not in the mood today. I decide to see if Taylor is working; hope she didn't get into trouble losing her card. I head over to Papi's.

I sit outside, and Joe makes me a Tom Collins. Another beautiful day of beachgoers. Couples all around. You can pick out the ones who are here for sex and which ones are here for relaxation. I don't see the bachelorettes from yesterday. Maybe the wedding is going on right now. Feeling alone again, I take my drink on a walk toward the beach; a few minutes in the sun won't hurt. My God, that couple is really going at it. I try not to look like I'm looking. His hands are all over her boobs while the waves come in over them. She laughs and swats him away. Let me guess: in about two hours they will be tired from all of the frolicking in the sun. They'll go to their room to shower, followed by dinner at The Flamingo, and back to their room for more fun. My mind is turning over. *Paul, Paul, you are not going to do that again … but it would be so easy. Let's just see if I'm right.* I take a chair over to my tree and sit in the shade with another drink. I get out my phone and make it look like I'm looking at it. With my sunglasses on, I watch the couple. She has on a blue bikini, is very petite, and has a loud voice. Her hair is brown and long. He is a foot taller than her and quite muscular. He has a better tan than she does; probably lifts weights outside, where lots of people can see him.

I wonder if one of them is cheating. If so, it would totally be him. He doesn't smile much, and she seems happy. He has something else on his mind: money, wife, job, or when he can work out again. Almost 4:00 p.m. now, and they are gathering up their belongings. Yep, I was right — it's almost two hours since I began watching them. My legs set in motion. *What are you doing?* I drag the chair back and set my glass on the bar.

I head to the lobby elevators from the inside hallway. I stop to look at some flyers in the rack while I see if they come this way. My heart is racing at the sight of them, now very close to me. The smell of sweat and ocean gleam off of them. I keep some flyers in my hand and enter the elevator with them. I push the button for the top floor. On the eighth floor, they get out. They are in front of me, and again I wait for a moment to step off. She's talking about how the shower will feel so good. I pop into the vending room. I hear their door open while I glance down the hall. When it closes, I slide by to verify the number, 814. I walk down the stairs at the end of the hall to confirm where I might be later on.

You can't do this again. What if you get caught and your family and coworkers find out what you were doing? Can you live with your mom and sister knowing about this? Jail is a real possibility. This guy could kill you with one punch. I know, I know, but I feel so alive. I'm concealed; I'm just a fly on the wall nobody will see, a troll under the bridge, or your biggest nightmare. I head outside and start walking up the block because I need to clear my head and think rationally. I pass a putt-putt golf shop and then a CVS. Resorts are all around, with people enjoying life together. I need to experience life again; one last hurrah before the summer is over. *One more time, just one more time, and then I'll throw away the card.* It will give me one more crazy memory to feel like I lived a little. I decide to eat something now, so that it will be digested by the time the show starts.

5

I HAVE DECIDED TO CALL them "Ken and Barbie." After an early dinner, I sit quietly in the lobby behind a magazine again. They reemerge, but they do not head into The Flamingo. My stomach is in knots just looking at them. She has her hand wrapped around his tree-trunk arm. This will surely be entertaining later on. Barbie is wearing the little black dress with black high heels, and her hair is pulled up with a few strands hanging down in front. Ken has on blue jeans with a blue-and-pink Hawaiian shirt. A big flashy watch on his right wrist. Not the best look together, but they are pretty, so it doesn't matter. Ken holds the door open for her as they leave the resort and walk up the street. I probably have at least two hours to waste. 814. Room 814. The anticipation is escalating.

The sun has gone down, so I decide to walk along the beach — one last time to talk myself out of what I am about to do again. Most people are having dinner or running the kids around. Not me. I am thinking about creeping to the highest degree. The beach is nearly empty, which is refreshing. As much as I want some connection, I don't want stares. I should start a private island for people who look different, with an abnormality of some sort. Where no one stares or points or prejudges. We could manufacture something cool, and we could all work together. I would be president, with my own personal jet on my personal runway. I should first start out with a blog and see how it goes. "Paul's Blog" has a ring to it, maybe "Paul's Anomaly Blog." That's it; I feel like I am meant for something better than washing dishes. *Just one more crazy night, and then I will start my blog. No more creeping after this. Just one more time.*

After all of this walking, my legs will be ready to just be still. I hydrate with some water and decide to head up. It will give me time to snoop, anyway. As I arrive on the eighth floor, a family walks past me at the elevator. Of course, I get the usual gawks and silence. I walk down the hall, past Room 814. All is quiet, while the nerves in my stomach claw at me. I picture Ken and Barbie in the room — way too interesting to pass up. I turn at the end of the hall and head back. I stop at the door, glance around, and listen. The key slides in, and I am inside. I smell an abundance of fragrance, like musk. Ken is a little over the top with his tan and smells. I start in the bathroom: makeup, brush, comb, toothbrushes/paste, deodorants, tanning oil, Tommy Musk, and long, brown hair all over the sink. Nothing interesting.

I see a large girl-bag on the floor. My heart starts to flutter now. Look at these tiny underwear and one pink bra. They are all very lacy and stringy. If my fingers could only feel perfectly. I bring them all to my nose and smell — amazing. A smell like I have never known. A little perfumey but a lot of body scents. I decide to keep one pair in my pocket, since this is the last time I am ever going to do this. She will miss the black pair, but these little pink ones look plain. I fold one carefully and place it in my pocket. I suppose that makes me an official pervert. The little dresses and bikinis are a mess in the bag. Not much else there.

I stand and go around the bed, toward his bag. *Why not?* It's on the desk. I glance in, and the clothes are folded neatly. Then I see something strange. It is a circuit board and another circuit board underneath it. There is a screwdriver and some rolls of wire. Why would he have this in a hotel room? Perhaps I will find out when I hear them talk. That's all part of the real-life, fly-on-the-wall experience. I get to be a part of their lives for a while and find out what they are doing here. Judge them and listen to crazy hotel sex. All fun and games from under the bed, I smile. Well, I look all around again and then behind the bed drape. Looks clean enough, again open and empty. I go to the bathroom to pee one last time. I wouldn't mind some more water, but I'd better not. I turn my phone off this time and check for my room card, car keys, panties, and now I am ready for the descent. I lie along the top, like before, and make sure everything is folded back down like a pro. Glad I don't smell like grease this time, but no one could smell it over the musk, anyway.

While I wait, my mind wanders to my sister, Tammy. She would be the one person who could understand me being under this bed. She grew up seeing me isolated, lonely, made fun of. If my mom knew what I was doing, she would be horrified; she tried to make everything pleasant. Mom thought people accepted me and were all understanding because she did. Funny how people are nice around her, but as soon as she was out of the room, the sneers and pointing began. Food thrown, laughing, gawking, but the worst part was the leaving. I could deal with the pointing and the laughing, but I hated the leaving. Tammy would sit by me when she could, but she played with her one little friend. I could never play with them. Now that I think of it, Tammy didn't play with her friend very much. Where was she? I don't remember what she was doing while I was feeling sorry for myself. Her bedroom was very plain. She was quiet growing up. Did she resent me because of the attention I got from Mom? I think it's time to take a trip home and see them. My niece, Jamie, loves to read and play Yahtzee. That sounds good. I wonder if Tammy and Johnny are dating now or not. I wonder what Johnny would say about me being under here — I have no idea. I still have time to get out. *Paul, are you going to take this chance again?* I envision the door opening and them coming in ... yes, one more time. Do I need to pee again? No, I'm good.

Now I think about the worms under my bed, because, now, *I'm* the worm under a bed. Mom would not yell at me. She would just get the sweeper out once in a while and suck them up after she scraped their dried-up bodies up from the carpet. I am just a big, thick, wrinkly worm now. Hiding under the bed, where it's dark. Waiting to crawl out at the right time;

hoping I don't dry up and die first. This is becoming a long wait, but, hopefully, well worth the effort.

I realize the fact that I don't ever sneeze is a good thing in this situation. With half of my nose gone and no hair, there is nothing to give me the need to sneeze. I don't remember what a sneeze feels like. An interesting freak fact is that I don't need a nose to smell. Scents travel to the olfactory cleft at the top of the nasal cavity, and scent cells are renewed every few months. My mom was so happy I didn't lose my sense of smell. I'm glad I did not breathe in the chili.

I should have put extra lotion on today. Taking a walk in the sun and not working in the humid kitchen has dried me out some. I don't itch, but I feel a little tight. I try to rub out some of the tightness. How much longer? I decide to get up and use the bathroom again and get a little drink. A nice little stretch and a couple jumps. I look in Ken's bag again, puzzled by the circuit boards. We all have our hobbies. He doesn't need porn for his hobby, because Ken has Barbie. Another little drink and a few more power jumps. I look at the door — last chance to change my mind — and I go back into the worm hole.

This time, while waiting, I think about my father. Were he and Tammy close? I know he was not close to me, but what about her? I don't remember. Did he do things with her? I do remember them playing hide-and-seek. Where was she when I had all of Mom's attention?

Finally, I hear someone. I don't hear any giggling. Something gets slammed down, and someone goes into the bathroom and shuts the door. Ken's powerful steps walk over to his bag, and he is quiet. I hear him mumble to himself and then say the word "God" louder. He does not sound happy. Then he walks toward the bathroom.

"Kelsey, I'm sorry. I was not flirting with her — we were just talking!" Silence. "I am very social with a few drinks in me; it's not a big deal. Are you going to come out soon, or do I have to find another bathroom to piss in?" She opens the door.

"I would never talk to other men and touch their hair if I was dating someone," she yells. Wow, this part is never in the adult movies. There were never arguments or fights of any kind that I can remember. There may not be any sex tonight; that's a disappointment.

"I didn't touch her hair, did I? I'm sorry. It didn't mean anything. You can't be mad over that, and we haven't even talked about commitment. We're just here to have a good time, so let's have a good time."

"We're here together — that's commitment enough to not be flirting. This is not just a game; maybe I shouldn't be doing this with you. I need to go." I hear her getting her things from the bathroom and putting them in her bag.

"Kelsey, come over here, and we can talk about it. I said I was sorry. It'll never happen again." They are now both sitting on the bed. "What can I do to convince you to stay?"

"Look, it's been real, but we don't seem to have that much in common, anyway. I can get a bus ride home from here, and we can stop what we're doing. I think that's best."

"You think that's *best*, huh? Little Miss Kelsey thinks that's *best*. Well, I didn't fork out the money for this room and your fancy dinner for you to run out of here. We have a lot at stake, and I don't think you're going anywhere!"

Now there is silence again. I have no idea what to think about this situation. This does not seem like the couple I saw today. No commitment? *Kelsey, what are you doing?* Why do girls do this? Meet someone, start having sex in hotels. I cannot imagine my sister or Taylor doing anything like this. Beth, maybe. Please, Kelsey, just get out — he sounds mad. I feel someone get up. Then I hear and feel a bounce on the bed.

"Stop it, Adam! Get off me!"

"You're not leaving me here, princess." His voice is calm, while I hear some panic in hers. "Are you going to calm down?" The struggling has stopped. She would be no match for him, unless she is possibly a black belt.

"Fine, let's talk," Kelsey says, staying calm. *Smart girl.*

"Now I have got to take a piss, and you're going to stay here; then we can talk." I hear him take something into the bathroom with him and set it down, probably her phone and purse. She is still on the bed. The intensity seems to have subsided. "Kelsey, remember we're going to the aquarium tomorrow. I'm sorry, okay?" I hear him talking from the bathroom and then a flush. He walks out. She is not talking. I would be mad about that "princess" comment he made.

"Adam, I would like to leave now. There doesn't have to be any trouble. Then you can go back to the bar and talk to that girl again." She stands and goes to the bathroom. She must be getting the rest of her things together. Oh, God. I want to soak into the floor and into the next room. Please just let her go.

H E TAKES A DEEP BREATH. I can feel Ken, or Adam,
getting mad again. I can smell his hate and tension from
under here; the room breathes hostility. She is moving about;
shuffling through her bag now.

"Let's look for a movie and watch it with some popcorn,"
he says calmly. He is trying hard to convince her to stay, but
she remains quiet for a minute.

"Thank you, Adam, for the education. You're great, but
I think our time together is done." *She is not going to change
her mind, big man — just let her go.* I am wishing I was never
here. "Sick to my stomach" would be a grand understatement.
Tears are coming out of my good eye. My body is too frozen to
even wipe them away. Fear for this girl, Kelsey, is consuming
me. Adam feels like a volcano ready to blow or a bull ready
to charge. She knows it too. If I jumped out from under this
bed, she might be able to leave while he pummels me, or I

could yell for her to get out, and it would take the focus off of her. My body is, however, frozen. I find it hard to breathe; it is stifling under here, and I am so close to them that it feels tangible. I could grab his feet, and he would fall down, just like in a horror movie. He would be pulled under the bed like a sack of potatoes never to be seen again. But this is no movie, and I am not a killer.

"Leave your shit alone!" Adam demands. "We are not *done*," he pronounces loudly. "No little princess is going to leave me here all alone. Who do you think you are?"

"I will scream if you touch me — I swear!"

"I will stuff your mouth full of my dirty shorts if you do," he replies with a sly twist to his voice. She grabs her bag and moves for the door. He moves too. "Oh, no, you don't," he demands. She screams loudly, but he quickly covers her mouth with something. Then there's a crash onto the bed with some thrashing. "Ouch, you bitch!" he yells. Then I hear a slap. She must have bit him. Even I could feel that slap. She cries, and I can feel the struggling. She is trying to scream, but she is muffled out. There is still thrashing above me, but it's more controlled. Then I hear Adam speak calmly.

"Don't worry. I'll take you home. You live by the river, right?" *Oh, my God — he has a pillow over her face now. He's killing her!* I picture my father being taken out of our house in a body bag. Was it because of me? Seeing my face every day. His son, me, unable to be a normal, "Let's play ball," or "Where are your friends?" kind of son. I picture Kelsey being taken out of here in a body bag. I have to do something. I slide out from under the bottom of the bed to peek over the bottom edge. He is straddling her, facing the top of the bed and, sure enough, with a pillow over her face. I stay down behind Adam. She is still struggling, but not as much. *Oh, my God; he's big. He will have to kill us both now.* I'm standing behind him, looking around for what to do. There is no way to stop this. Then I turn around and see his bag; I remember the screwdriver inside. I reach in and grab it. *Paul, you only have one shot here to stop him.*

I take a deep breath and step on the bed beside him, wrap myself around his back like a monkey, and plunge the screwdriver into his neck on his other side with all of the force my right arm has. I hold it in place while clinging to his upper back and wrap my left arm around his neck. He has already released the pillow and jerks up. He easily lifts me along with him. I see Kelsey gasping for breath and crawling toward the top of the bed. Thank God she's alive, but so is Adam. I think I feel warmth running over my hand and arm. I keep a firm hold of the handle and his neck, and my legs are wrapped around him now like a vise. I cannot let him get to me. He tries to pull my arms away from his neck, but the sight of his own blood must have him puzzled as to what has happened to him. He backs up away from the bed. Some awful gagging and groans are coming from him. *You're dead, big guy, and you know it. There is nothing to stop this from happening, and nothing will knock me off of you.* I'm not sure if he is more terrified about someone on his back or the blood pooling on the floor. He stumbles sideways.

He drops to his knees soon after that, still groaning. I keep my legs around him. Kelsey is hiding now and looking at me with fear. I look at her, pleading — without using any words — for her to not be scared of me. Ken then goes all the way down just as I pull my legs out from around him. He is still making hollow gasps. His face and neck are bluish in color, and the carpet is turning bright red. The bed and floor look like that horror movie that I'm in now — and I'm the killer. I let go of him, and he is silent, face down beside her bag — now sprayed with blood. I move to the wall behind me and sit with my arms over my head and bent-up knees. The smells are strong: blood, copper, sweat, and fear. We are both silent. The hallway is silent. I can't cry or talk or look at her now. She must feel the same way.

After what seems like minutes, she starts crying. I look up at her, hoping I do not scare her. She is holding a pillow to her body, crouched at the top of the bed, looking at me. I decide to talk to her, because there is no getting out of this.

"I'm Paul. Are you okay?" She says nothing. I look at my hands, covered in blood, along with most of my right arm. "I'm going to go into the bathroom to wash myself up some. You might want to call the front desk and have the police come." I slowly stand up and walk to the restroom. I hear her pick up the phone and dial one number.

"I, I, I … Room 814. I need the police to come up here. There's a dead body," she talks through her cracked voice and tears. I can't wash all of this off without a shower and clothes to put on. I sit on the edge of the shower with my head down. I can't look at myself in the mirror. My family is going to find out about this: my mom, my sister, and my grandparents. I will probably lose my job and have to move away. What if the police try to put me in jail for murder? Panic starts to set in. I thought my life was bad before; what word is worse than "freak"? Now "a perverted, murdering freak." My poor mom.

I think of Kelsey still on the bed. *What is she thinking? Here I am, thinking about myself again, when this girl was nearly killed. She's quiet, and I'm numb with the events that just happened a few feet from me. Can I run away?* Then there is a knock at the door, and whoever is out there lets themselves in. There stand three men in suits, looking at the dead man and blood all over the floor. They look at me in the bathroom and see Kelsey, I am guessing, on the bed.

"Miss, are you who called us? I need both of you to stay right where you are until the police get here." They move back to the hallway and keep the door partway open; I hear them whispering. Not good for the hotel guests to see this mess. With my head in my hands, I break down and cry. I should have run out of this room after he dropped. I could have disappeared, but she saw my face. People around here would know who the freak-faced mystery man was. Never saw this ever happening in my fantasy. They were just on the beach having fun; how did this materialize? My poor mom. What is she going to say? My fate could be in this poor girl's hands. I'm terrified now; nausea overwhelms me, and I retch into the toilet. I wash myself in the sink again, trying to get more blood off my arms. I can't look at myself. I never want to see me again.

The police arrive. One puts on a glove and bends down to check for a pulse. The screwdriver is still in his neck.

"We need to take statements from both of you and then go down to the station until all of this is sorted out. Do you both understand? My name is Officer Corbin, and this is Officer Chuck. I'll talk to the guy in the bathroom, if you want to talk to her," he says to Officer Chuck. Corbin is very tall, with a kind face; he takes charge of the situation. He comes into the bathroom and shuts the door. I guess he doesn't want anyone to hear.

"Sir." He looks at me and is wondering what I am. "First, I need your name and your statement on what happened here." I sit on the shower ledge now; he remains standing. He is looking around the bathroom now. "Whenever you're ready," he states firmly. I don't really know how to tell him anything.

"My name is Paul Duram. I don't even know the man or the girl. The man was killing the girl by smothering her with a pillow, so I jumped on his back and stopped him with the screwdriver. That's all I know." I face the floor. I can't even think about all of the ways my life is going to change now.

"If you don't know them, how did you know he was smothering her?"

"I was hiding under the bed, and they didn't know I was in the room." That stopped his questioning.

"Paul, we're going to take you down to the station now. I need you to come along with me." I stand up and walk past him. I don't even look toward the bed. I just walk out; I can't face her. I feel like I'm never going home again. My island sounds real good right about now. He leads me to the parking lot.

In the police cruiser, the driver stares at me in the rear-view mirror, while sitting in the back. Officer Corbin goes back inside. The driver occasionally clears his throat, but no words are said as we drive away. There is blood around my nails and in the creases of my scars. Now I know that my skin *can* look even worse. After we reach the station, I am led into a room, and I sit down in one of the chairs. There's a table and another chair, just like the TV shows. I am offered some water, and I accept. It is hard to drink with my stomach in knots, but I am parched. After a half hour goes by, I ask for more water. Nobody has come in to talk to me. There's a big window, behind which I'm sure people are standing on the other side, studying me. They told me not to use my phone while in here. I lay my head down on my arms. Thoughts of my mom come back. Maybe no one will have to know. This could easily be cleared up, and I could be on my way. What is Kelsey saying? I need to be that fly on the wall again. What was I thinking? My life was complicated enough. *Well, Paul, you wanted an adrenaline rush. How does it feel? The freak is behind the display case now; bring in the clowns and elephants.*

Officer Corbin opens the door and startles me. He pulls out the other chair and sits down. He has some papers in front of him. I am so nauseous.

"Paul," he begins, "we have talked to Kelsey, and she corroborates what you said. She has rub abrasions across her face, consistent with smothering under a pillow. The man you killed has scratches on his arms from Kelsey, and she has blood under her fingernails. What we don't understand is you. Please explain to me in detail how you were in this room and why."

Where do I even start? Tears are forming on my good side again. I hide my face in my hands, and emotion takes over. My ability to talk has left me as I sit in a police station and face the inevitable consequences. I have never been in trouble before; my sheltered life has not prepared me for defending myself. My mother was the defender while I was just covered away. How is this normal-looking person going to understand what I describe?

Officer Corbin says, "I understand this has been a bad night for you, but please try to explain. Kelsey wanted me to tell you thank you, if that helps, but she is also confused." I look up at him, and I do feel better hearing that. He gets me some more water, and I drink it. He stares at me, waiting.

I begin: "I was hiding under the bed, because I wanted to experience a connection with people in real life." Officer Corbin waits for more. "When I'm around most people, they will stare or leave or just become silent. It was just for some excitement in my life, or like an experiment. Then, when they started fighting, it all changed. I was terrified for the girl and for myself. I realized he was killing her, so I had to do something. I got out from under the bed and got behind him; I felt that I had to make sure I stopped him. The screwdriver was the best thing I could think of and I jumped on his back while ... well, you saw." He stares at me.

"Where did you get the screwdriver?"

"I saw it in his bag before they arrived back to their room. I was snooping around." I put my hands in front of my face again. "I'm so embarrassed." I feel the tension roll on.

"How did you enter their room?" he asks.

"I stole a room key from a coworker who cleans the rooms. I work at the resort at Papi's restaurant."

He sits back in his chair and takes a deep breath. I can feel his movements and stares. He gets up and leaves me here alone

OUT OF THE WORMHOLE

again. It feels worse to be alone. I feel like a broken animal in a cage, but much worse than my normal brokenness. I wish I could just wake up from this nightmare. I keep imagining what would have been warm ooze running over my hands and hearing his groans in my ears. I feel the slow fall of the monster trying to figure out how he became the prey. I saved the girl; can I just go home now ... please?

7

I WAIT FOR WHAT SEEMS LIKE hours. Officer Corbin comes back in.

"I spoke with the resort manager, and, of course, you are no longer employed there. He does not want to press any charges against you since you have been a model employee. I will need the room key card from you for evidence. Kelsey Raymond is the girl you saved tonight in this strange turn of events. She does not want to press any charges against you for criminal trespass, and she would like to talk with you, if that's okay." I nod. He leaves again.

Shortly after that, she walks slowly into the room and closes the door. I watch her pull out the chair and sit down. She stares at me, and I see the redness on her nose, chin, and cheekbones. Her eyes are bloodshot, and she looks scared and at a loss for words. I realize she probably sees the dried blood on my arms and my shirt. She can't see my legs. There is quite a bit of dried blood on my right leg. I must look terrifying to her, so I try to smile.

"I just wanted to thank you for what you did. 'Paul,' is it?" she says. I nod. "If it wasn't for you, I wouldn't be here now, and … ummm …" Now she is crying, which makes me cry again. Oh, my God — I want to tell her I was so scared for her, but I can't speak. "Thank you," she says, wiping her nose with tissues. She gets up and leaves, just like that.

The other officer, Chuck, comes in now and asks me to follow him. He explains to me that they need to take my clothes; he hands me some scrub clothes to change into. I also give him the hotel key. Then I remember the panties folded up in my front pocket. Nausea again. In the bathroom stall, I change my clothes and take everything out of my pants. Surprised they didn't search me. I flush the panties down the toilet in case they still want to search me. I have my car keys and phone. I hand him my clothes when I emerge. They also want my shoes. I'm wearing scrubs and socks; Chuck leads me to another room.

"We're going to take your fingerprints and photo just because of the circumstances. I'm sure you understand." I nod. A lady fumbles with my fingers with her plastic gloves on and is noticeably uncomfortable and mystified by the strange marks left on the paper. No fingerprints to be seen. They do each finger anyway. After that, they want to see my driver's license and take some photos of me from all sides. They ask for my phone number, address, and next of kin; they tell me I need to stay in the area until I'm told I can leave. I hear Officer Chuck say words like "burglary," "aggravated criminal trespass," and "manslaughter," but that they feel no charges will be filed. "I'll drive you home or to your car now." Officer Chuck leads me with his hands through two more doors.

"I need to go back to the resort to get my car," I explain. No more words are said. I am so happy to be going home and hoping this is all done.

When we arrive, I point to where my car is, and he has to get out to let me out of the car.

"Thank you," I tell him.

"Remember, we will be talking to you some more soon, so stick around." I get into my car and watch him pull away. I look around the lot. I see that it is two thirty-five in the morning when I pull out my phone and check for messages. I turn on the ringer and see that nobody has called or sent a text — the usual. The parking lot is lit up, and I can see that Papi's is closed down and dark. I no longer work here. I will no longer see Joe or Beth or Brandon or Taylor. They are my only friends here, and they will hear about this. What will they think? Maybe it will just be the hotel staff, and my family will never have to find out. I sit here in the car, looking toward my tree and the beach view I used to treasure.

Can I even drive right now? My head is spinning, and I can't concentrate. This late at night, there probably are not many cars. *This is just as good a time as any — just get home.* Both hands clutching the wheel and trying to focus on the traffic lights and signs, I drive slowly toward the swamplands where I live. I drive across the bridge over the Waccamaw Refuge, but it feels different now. The darkness and the swampy depth are closer to me. The alligators are down there, waiting for me now, because I need to be punished. Cameras are everywhere, watching me, waiting for me to screw up or to see what I will do next. The darkness will swallow me up next time, a real wormhole. Just one more foot off the cliff, and I will fall. The freak will be dead at last. Everyone will be relieved.

I pull up to my trailer and go inside. No woodpeckers. Silence. The silence does not help. I turn on some music, strip down, and get into the shower. The blood had soaked through my pants and dried on my thigh. I will run out of hot water before I scrub this all off. Once the water turns cold, I get out. I sit up on the side of my bed, safely terrified. Being next to a bed suddenly sickens me. I go to the couch and sit down. Music is playing, something from Miranda. I wonder what Kelsey is doing now. Did she call her parents? Is she going back to the river? What river does she live by? Does she also feel closer to the darkness now? She was nearly killed, and that has to change a person.

I never do fall asleep. I spend the rest of the night staring at the wall. I have a picture above my TV of my sister and niece together in a pose. It was taken about three years ago. Little Jamie is sitting in a chair, and Tammy is behind her. They look very similar; Tammy could be sisters with Sandra Bullock. We are all thin, with dark hair. I know that, if I wasn't covered in burn scars, I would have been handsome. My one good eye and hair on my right side are very nice when everything else is covered up. I wish Kelsey could just see that much of me. *I'm really not a mutant under your bed; I'm a nice guy.* She will surely have nightmares about men attacking her, men under her bed, or men stalking her. I feel bad about that, but is it possible her life will become better, since she's alive?

The sun is coming up and I hear commotion outside. I look out the window and see the WMBF News van outside, and there is a knock on my door. Oh, my God! How did they know about this? I suppose from the staff at Bayliner's. I hear someone say my name.

"Paul, Paul Duram — this is Mandy Brown with your local news. Can you come out and answer a few questions for us?" I freeze in place. There is no way I am answering the door to them. This is not going to just go away, is it? I have to keep my family from knowing I was hiding under a bed in a hotel room. I smack my head. *Stupid, stupid, stupid.*

"Paul?" She's not leaving. I hide behind the door, not two feet from where they are standing. Just go away. I'm not coming out. If I move, they could hear me. If they look through the window, they could almost see me, so I stand right up against the door. The woodpeckers are also knocking to get in. So much noise after hours of silence. Please leave me alone.

I can now hear them talking to my neighbor.

"Do you know Paul, ma'am? Hi, I'm Mandy. I hope we're not disturbing you this morning." I hear Bonnie talk. Bonnie hardly ever comes outside. She is nice enough to me. Quiet when I am around, like most people. Once she helped me with my laundry when I dropped my clean wet clothes all over the ground. She said, "Don't touch the dirt; just hang the clothes up to dry, and then the dirt will beat right out of them." She was right.

"Well, his car is here. Guess he just doesn't want to talk to you," Bonnie tells her. That makes me smile a little bit. *Make them leave, Bonnie — you can do it.*

"Do you know Paul very well? Sorry — what is your name?"

"No, I don't," she answered. "I'm not interested in an interview, either." I hear Bonnie's door open and shut. *Take the hint, Mandy.* Then I hear the van's doors slam, and the news van turns around to leave. Relief. I wonder what people at work are going to hear or say about me. I picture Taylor realizing I stole her key. I slide down the door until I am sitting on the floor, totally ashamed.

I fear someone else may come, so I decide to leave while I can. I grab my car charger, some drinks, sandwich, cookies, and a bag of Doritos. I also decide to grab a blanket and my emu lotion. If Bonnie comes out, I will thank her, but she doesn't. I drive over to the public entrance of the Waccamaw National Wildlife refuge and drive to a quiet place far back to park, surrounded by thirty thousand acres of cypress trees, eagles, woodpeckers, and alligators. After walking a while, I find a shady spot and throw everything down. What's my next move? Moving will be my next move. I lay the blanket out and then myself. I put some lotion on; my skin is overly dry from all the events of last night. Only water tastes good, and a couple bites of my sandwich. I make a mental list of calls I need to make: tell landlord this will be my last month living here; call Mom and tell her I have decided to move; call grandparents; maybe ask sister if I can crash with her for a while. I can't just run back to mommy, but my sister and I are not very close, either. We were close when we were young, but, as we got older, living in the same house is as close as it got. While thinking about my next move and listening to the woodpeckers just above my head, I fall asleep, not even considering the alligators.

8

I SLEEP FOR ABOUT four hours. My eyes open to a new point of view, a new favorite spot. No missed calls on my phone. Hopefully, my family will never hear about this. I rethink my idea of going to my sister's house; she will know something is going on, with her questioning face and silence. Tammy has a way of making people uncomfortable around her; I just avoid her most of the time. How much money do I even have now? How soon will I need to find a job? My checking account has around $600 and my savings account less than that. That will not last long unless I live out of my Elantra. I think about my other grandparents, Tom and Sandy. They go to the Florida Keys this time of year after the Mackinaw Island tourism is done. There is a pullout couch in their camper, and I could stay there. I could find another beach, another dishwashing job, and a new trailer. I will just need a new hobby. Looking at girls in bikinis does not sound that appealing anymore. Sex seems bad, my movies sound awful, and the hotter weather would be a challenge to my skin. *A plan, Paul — we need a plan here.*

I am finally getting hungry. I eat some of the food I brought. Hopefully nobody is waiting for me at home, because I need to prepare. In my car, I have to concentrate on driving; my eyes feel like I am looking into a tunnel. My thoughts are sporadic, and my movements are jittery. I am a different person. I took a life; it was an evil life, but I took it. I never thought that I would have to face a bigger challenge than my normal existence.

I park, get out, and run straight into my little box. It feels smaller, not safe. I jump at the knock on the door.

"Paul, it's Bonnie. I need to talk to you." She sounds concerned, and I hear her coughing a few times. I open the door. "Can I come in?" I step aside. She has never come in before. I see her looking around, holding her hands together like she is anxious. *Oh, God — what?* "Let's sit down at the table," she says. I have a small table with two chairs by a window. We sit. She is hesitant to tell me anything.

"Did someone else come by?" I ask.

"No, I was watching the news this morning, and there was a story from a hotel." My stomach drops out and my breathing becomes difficult. I try to stay composed. "It was a quick blurb about a woman almost killed in a hotel room, but an employee saved her because he was stalking them under their bed. It said the employee's a recluse burn victim. Then they made a joke about checking under the bed next time." She is looking right at me now, but without any judgment. I can see compassion in her eyes. "I figured it must be you when they mentioned 'burn victim.' Is that really what happened?" I close my eyes, realizing my fate is sealed now. Life will never be the same — the freak stalker in the news media.

"Well, it is somewhat true. Yes, I was under the bed, but I was just wanting to feel close to people. Get a high. A one-time thing, but then he started hurting her and trying to kill her. I had to stop him." My reaction is not to cover my face this time but to look at her for a reply. Does she understand? Can anyone understand that I am not really a creeper, but curious? Is there a difference? I hope my grandparents were not watching the local news this morning. Hopefully, they were at the store early and working on some little sharks or something. I picture them hearing about this story. They will be mortified. My mom ... yep, I can't live with any family. "I lost my job." She smiles.

"Paul, you saved a girl's life. That is what you need to think about. I'm sure people will also focus on you under the bed, but you need to remember that poor girl."

"My family is going to find out ... what'll they think?" She is silent. I cannot look at her now.

"I don't know how to help you there. You'll just have to be honest." There is nothing she can say that will help. "I'm going to go now. I'm sure it will all work out. Tomorrow, there will be another story."

"Bonnie, thanks for coming over and talking to me. I'll be moving soon; without my job and this story, I can't stay in this town now." She nods and lets herself out. Before she shuts the door, she mentions she wouldn't mind leaving too. I watch her go back to her trailer. *What does that mean?*

As much as I want to run, I am mentally and physically exhausted. I fall onto the couch. I check my phone, because I did hear some texts come in while driving home. It is Grandpa Ed, asking me to call him. They must have seen the news. There is also a missed call from Taylor. I wonder if she's mad. I place the phone on the side table, beside my lamp made out of shells with a little shark. I made it when I first moved here and hung out over at Hook's more often. This is not a good time to call anyone back. The story needs to settle down for a few days; then it will be easier to talk about. It's too soon. I feel myself plunging the screwdriver in and seeing the look in Kelsey's eyes. How is Kelsey now? Is she back home with her family — not alone, like me? Will she remember me as the guy who saved her life or the guy under her bed?

I close my eyes. The police told me not to go anywhere yet. Well, that's just great. What am I waiting for? Complete social degradation?

My phone ringing wakes me out of my trance. It's Mom. Well, I must get this over with. I answer.

"Paul, are you alright? I am hearing of something happening down there from your grandma. Are you the one on the news?"

"Yes, Mom. I'm sorry I didn't call you right away. It's still sinking in for me."

"So you did kill someone while saving a girl?"

"Yes."

"And you were hiding under the bed? I don't understand."

"I know. I don't know if you can understand, Mom."

"I'm listening." She hears my silence. "I think I'm just going to come down there now."

"No, Mom. Listen, I'll be moving soon, and I'm leaving most of this stuff here. I don't want any of this old stuff left from other people. I don't know when or where, but I'll let you know when I know. I'm just not allowed to leave yet." I stand my ground. I can't have my mommy saving me this time.

"Okay. I won't come right now, but please explain what you were doing."

"I just wanted to be with people acting normally and be a part of their lives. You know how people are in front of me. I had this crazy idea about being a fly on the wall. I thought what I was doing was having some stupid fun. Never meant to get caught in their lives or hurt anyone. Then ... well ... you heard ... right?"

"How did you kill this man?"

"I don't want to talk about it, Mom. Not now. I just want to get past this." I feel the emotions rising up my throat.

"Okay, okay, but I think I need to be there. You need someone with you."

"I have Pap and Mo if I do. I might even be driving back to Michigan soon, alright? Let's just let this blow over, please."

"I still don't understand all of this; have you done that before, this under-the-bed thing?"

"No." No one needs to know any different. She is wanting me to talk more. "I will call you later today, okay?

"Alright. Be sure you do. I love you honey."

"Goodbye, Mom," I say. Back to a fetal position on the couch.

The sandwich and chips are not sitting well as I just stare at my little world. This couch came with the trailer. I just bought a cover to put over it. The bed also came with it. Gross. The table and chairs were also here, along with the pots and pans. I only bought some cups, plates, towels, and a bottle of all-purpose cleaner. The little grill outside is cheap and rusty. I need to take only my clothes in my laundry basket. I do like the towels. Is that all? Is that all I have in life? Towels? I will need to find a cheap place to live. The rent and cost of food is high here, close to the beach; that is where most of my money goes. At least my car is good. I also own those stupid adult movies. My private escape, which is probably what led me to do this in the first place. I don't even want them anymore; that will be the first thing to go. Especially before the police decide to come and search my place, looking for more perverted evidence. I jump up, get a trash bag, and empty out my closet stash of porn. I grab my keys and head to the nearest gas station. I drive by the back dumpster and throw them in.

Now what? I am used to going to work around this time, enjoying my view for a while before starting the day's cleanup. My previous life is done and gone. I think about my "island of the misfits" again. Making the toys and drinking piña coladas all day. That sounds good. Everyone can just let their disfigure hang out and flaunt it. I actually smile at the thought.

Life does feel better in the daylight; it gives it a whole new feel since last night. Of course, I am not covered in blood and driving home from an interrogation, either. The mind works differently in the daytime. The night casts a spell when it comes around. Darkness is threatening. Where do I want to be tonight? Here, at Grandpa's store, surrounded by fish, in my car, somewhere with people around me even if they aren't talking to me? Now I am dealing with self-preservation of whatever life is left for me. I drive back.

I walk outside and patrol around my camper. I picture people hiding behind my trailer waiting to ambush me or cars pulling up behind me and blocking me in. I need to get away from here. The first thing I do is call the lot manager and leave a message that I will be leaving by the end of the month. Am I really going to go back to Michigan and Mom? I can't do that, because Mom should not have to deal with this mess. She has done enough raising me and sheltering me from the ugly world. I brought this on myself, and I will have to live with it. Hopefully, I will be notified soon that all this has been put to rest, and I can go.

I contemplate going to the Florida Keys again. Maybe I should give them a call. Tom and Sandy Foraker are my mom's parents. I was never as close to them as I was to Dad's parents. Tom and Sandy didn't visit much while I was growing up. They are nice and all, but not as fun. Maybe Dad's parents felt like they had to make up for Dad leaving us. I am grateful for the family I have; I just hope they will all still love me.

I go back inside and look around the trailer again. What do I want to keep? There is an empty space in the closet now. I hate that empty space. What was I thinking? I think of the empty space under the beds and the individuals I encountered. I don't want to get to know other people after finding out how people really talk and treat each other behind closed doors. I'm not missing out on anything. *Focus on your life, Paul. You'll need money ... right ... yes, and you need work somewhere, alone, separated like always. Maybe I could work with animals.* Okay, I am feeling better concentrating on the future and not on today. I will get past today and tomorrow, and it will get better.

I will keep my sheets, towels, and pictures. That will all fit into a big box. I will take my clothes and my one pair of shoes left. Is that my life? Two boxes full? My phone rings; it is my sister. I can't talk to her right now. I don't want to have to explain myself again. What is this? In a drawer at the bottom of a built-in dresser, I find some old pictures and letters I kept. I have not looked at these things since I threw them in here. There are pictures of Mom and Dad together, birthday cards from family, high school diploma in a frame, and pictures of me after the burn. My small pile of keepsakes. I did not like my picture taken as I got older. Mom must have more at home, along with my birth certificate. I look so small and scared in the photos. I see some snapshots with visitors and me holding balloon animals in my bandaged hands. If I can live through that, I can live through this. Maybe I could volunteer with other burned kids, but will the world let me?

I hear tires-on-gravel again. I peek out the window, and the same news van pulls up. I quickly stand up against the door again. The inevitable knock across my backside.

"Paul, this is Mandy again. I understand you don't want to come out. I have a proposition for you, so I hope you can hear me. We would like to interview you and Kelsey. The public wants to hear more about this story, and you can tell your side. We will pay you two thousand dollars after the interview, and we can even blur your face if you want. I will leave my card here. I hope you decide to let us know about that night you saved a life. I will look forward to your call." Then they were gone.

I pick up the card and throw it onto the table. "Mandy Brown, WMBF News, morning anchor," along with phone number and email. "Two thousand dollars" does spark my interest. I wonder if Kelsey would be there; seeing her again sounds interesting, because now we have a shared experience that most people don't. Talking about what I did in a television interview does not sound like moving on, however. I really just want to know when I can get away from here.

I T HAS BEEN FOUR DAYS since the incident, and I'm still sleeping on the couch. Bonnie is sitting outside, looking my way with her morning java. I decide human contact would be good today. A shower with fresh clothes also sounds like a good idea. I get some water and a chair and head over to my neighbor. We sit in silence for a while.

"Are you going to do the interview?" she asks. I guess she could hear Mandy talking to me through the door. I have been rolling this around in my head. The money would be nice, and I would like to see Kelsey again. I feel a pull to see this girl again, and I want her to know I am not really a pervert. Was she more scared of him or me?

"I don't know." Do I tell my side before I leave this town forever? What do I have to lose? "Do you think I should?"

"Sure, you're a good person, and you should let the world know that. People are understanding when someone pours out their heart." Bonnie is convincing. I hear a car driving slowly in the gravel. A police cruiser pulls up behind my car. Officer Corbin gets out. Sickness takes hold.

"Good morning, Paul. Can we go inside and talk?"

"Sure," I answer. I leave my chair and tell my legs to stand up and open the door. He follows me in, and we sit at the table. He looks around, but it doesn't take him long to see everything.

"I want to let you know of some details. First, you are no longer required to stay here. Bayliner's does not want to press any charges against you, either. Both you and Kelsey's stories have been confirmed with the evidence we found at the scene. I'm sure you know that, if you're ever caught doing this little trick again, you will be prosecuted." I nod my head. "One more interesting thing. Adam worked for a security company. Kelsey was also working for them, and this is how they met. Adam had those circuit boards in his bag, and he was changing the programs in them before installing them into new clients' homes. After talking with Bang Security, they said clients were having problems with break-ins. Homeowners were routinely reporting that items were missing over a period of months. Nothing could be proven, but with the circuit panels in his possession, it's obvious he was tampering with them before installation. He was able to enter the homes when no one was there and take select items. Adam knew who had security cameras and who didn't. He worked for a computer company before Bang Security. He also lived well above his means, another clue. Adam had an elaborate scheme going on."

I was happy to hear all of this, especially the part about being free to go.

"How is Kelsey doing?" I ask.

"Hard to say. Very private. Bayliner's is letting her stay there until this is resolved. I haven't seen any family, and she refuses any counseling help. She doesn't let me into her room to talk to her; she wants to talk only by phone. I'm a little worried about her."

"Do you think I can help, since I was there and experienced this with her?"

"I don't know. Seeing you could possibly just remind her of the trauma," he explains nicely. "Do you have any questions for me?" I contemplate all that he said to me. Adam was a thief and a potential murderer. Crazy.

"A newswoman has come here a couple times, trying to get me to tell my story. Do you think I should do it?"

"That's your call, Paul. If you feel you need to. Are they paying you?"

"Yes."

"Well, maybe Kelsey will feel better if she talks about it. I don't really know." He stands up to leave. He puts his hand out to shake mine. I am not used to that gesture. I shake it back. "Thank you for saving a life, but find a different hobby." He smiles at me.

"I will." He leaves, and I go back out to my chair outside. "I am free to go," I tell Bonnie.

"That's great. Where will you go?" I shake my head, listening to the pounding on the wood.

"Somewhere without woodpeckers," I say with a smile. I decide at that moment that I will do the interview if Kelsey does it with me. We can get closure on this, and I can get some cash in my pocket.

"I'll miss you when you leave. You are a quiet neighbor, and you keep your stuff clean and picked up. I know you're a good person. I've got a daughter out in Minnesota. She's married with three kids. Never seems to have time to come here and visit. I sit and wait for her to call; when I call her, she's always too busy to talk."

I don't know what to say to this woman sitting next to me. People have never opened up to me before. I am having a real-life conversation with a nonfamily member. The police officer coming here could count as a conversation, but I don't think it does.

She goes on. "I had a son who died of an overdose several years ago. My husband is also dead." She coughs some and clears her throat. *She's lonely too.* I sit with her a while longer and then tell her I have to make some calls and that I would see her later.

I call Mandy and leave a message on her voicemail. I mention that I will do it only if Kelsey is there too. Me on TV; the thought makes me nervous. I will want to be blurred out, and I want the chance to tell people that I didn't hide under the bed for anything other than human connection. I spend the rest of my morning lying on the couch, waiting for a phone call and the next thing to happen, whatever that will be.

For lunch, I decide I want to go to Nathan's for hot dogs and ice cream. It might be my last time. I walk in to order.

People are staring, like always, but are they staring at *me* or as the person they heard about on the news? Am I being paranoid, or are more fingers pointing and whispers more pronounced? Another confirmation that I cannot stay here. I drive to Bayliner's and park far out in the lot; I eat my lunch in the car. I contemplate walking over to Papi's and seeing everyone, but my legs won't let me. I can't bring myself to see my old coworkers, friends, and job. I need to start a new chapter somewhere else. I decide to go to Hook's; I need to face family eventually.

I walk inside. There are no customers, and it's very quiet. I go to the back room, and they are both working on a large stingray. It is upside down, and Grandpa is painting the inner gills red while Grandma is trying to hold it still.

"Grab the other side, and hold it steady." I rush over and take some of the weight. Need to keep the head protected. We watch him expertly paint the red on it to make it look alive … I flash to the red coming out of Ken's neck and running down my hand, arm, and onto my leg. The plunge, the gurgling, the slow-motion takedown. I try to put that out of my head while I focus on holding still. I look up at the tools hanging neatly on the wall. I focus right on a screwdriver. Oh, God, I want to scream. How could that have happened? How could I have done that to another person? I try to remember what he was doing. *He was killing a girl, Paul — you saved her life and possibly your own. Close your eyes, and hold this dead fish. You are okay. Breathe. Keep it together.*

"Okay, put it down slowly with its head between these towels." Grandma and I worked slowly together, keeping the paint from running with any bumps of the head. Perfect. They both look at me. "It's about time you showed up," he says. I am still looking at that screwdriver. "Paul, come sit down. You look paler than normal." I sit down, and a tear forms in my stupid eye. Grandma leaves the room. Grandpa sits down with me.

"You take all the time you need, son. We are all letting you work this out in your own time." My head falls to my arms on the table, and I cry. I don't know where all of this came from, but it is coming out here with Grandpa Ed. He sits with me till I am done sobbing.

"I didn't want any of this to happen," I muster out.

"We know." He places a hand on my arm. "It's a shocking story to hear, and when you're ready, we'll talk about it."

"Is Grandma ashamed of me?"

"No, of course not. She's just worried." She can't face me — the freak under the bed; this breaks my heart. That settles it. I am looking forward to telling my story so people understand that I'm not really a perverted nightmare.

"I'm moving away from here," I say with a heavy heart.

"I figured you would. We'll miss seeing you around. We'll probably sell the shop in a few years. Find a nice place to live. Maybe we will come to you next time."

That's a nice thought, but I doubt that he's serious. I am good for nothing in most areas. Hands don't work very well, scare people off, and now clouded with peeping-Tom tendencies. Just what every grandparent wants to brag about.

"I'm working it out, and thank you for always being there for me, but I need to get away." He nods. I get up to leave. I don't see Grandma anywhere. I drive away.

That afternoon, I get a phone call from Mandy, the news anchor. She tells me that, tomorrow, an interview is set up with Kelsey and me together. We can tell our stories, and it will be broadcast the following day; two thousand dollars to each after the interview. I agree to be there at nine in the morning. I will leave town after that with my car packed and some money in my pocket.

I eat food out of my little freezer. Tonight, it is Stouffer's lasagna. Mom makes great lasagna with spicy sausage and ricotta cheese. I contemplate going home again. The thought of interrupting her life and having to look at her face, and wondering what she thinks about me are too much to deal with. The Florida Keys sounds like a plan, and it won't be overly hot with fall coming on. I have my other grandparent's phone number, so I'll call on my way down there. I will just stay on their couch till I find a place and a job.

There is a knock at the door. It's Bonnie. I tell her to come in.

"Paul, I know you are leaving soon. I just wondered where you're headed."

"I'm thinking about the Keys. I have family down there." She wants to ask me something. She clears her throat after she coughs from climbing up inside.

"Well, I was wondering if you wouldn't mind some company. I've got some money saved up. I don't know if you know this, but I can't drive because of my eyesight, and my lungs are bad. I am just stuck in this trailer every day till someone finds my stinking corpse. The thought of going somewhere new and getting away from this place would make an old woman so happy. One last hurrah. Don't answer me now — just think about it. We could both help each other out, and then neither of us would have to be alone. I'll get my own place, of course. I just want to get out of here."

I don't know what to say. This is very unexpected. Why would she want to go anywhere with me? Awkward moment.

"I'll think about it." She gets up and walks to the door. She is not a small woman and would take up some space. It would be nice not traveling alone, but I don't really know her. Not sure why she doesn't just call her daughter or take a bus somewhere. However, right now, Bonnie is actually the only friend I have in this world. She trudges back over to her outside chair. Still, that all sounds weird; what would I do with her at my grandparents' place? I can't think about that right now. I contemplate calling Taylor and telling her I am sorry, but I can't bring myself to do it. I will just text her "Hello" and that I am sorry … done.

10

A T 8:30 AM, I AM pacing in my trailer. Deep down, I know the main reason I am doing this is to see Kelsey again; otherwise, our paths would never cross. If there is anyone I want to explain myself to, it would be her. It's finally time to go for the interview, and my trunk is packed. I leave a note inside Bonnie's mailbox that I need to go alone and that she should call her daughter. I'm sure she'll understand.

The news station is up on a hill, with a small tower behind it; looks like the only hill around this area. As I walk in, I am immediately greeted by a young woman who seems to know exactly who I am.

"Hello, Paul. My name is Cindy. Please follow me to the set." I follow her through hallways with pictures of people all along the wall. Cindy is young and doesn't walk too close to me. She smells of a strong perfume and wears tight-fitting clothes. Then, we go into a large, open room that is darkened.

OUT OF THE WORMHOLE

Big pieces of old equipment are tarped over and collecting dust in the back of the room. There is a stage set up in the front, and we're walking toward it. When we arrive, I see Kelsey sitting in a chair, looking nervous. She looks thinner in the face and pale compared to when I saw her last. She is wearing black pants and a long-sleeved, pink, button-down shirt. Her hair is down. I wore my only pair of jeans and a long-sleeved shirt, also. This is as dressy as it gets and covers the most. Cindy has me sit down beside Kelsey. There are about ten other people in the room; most are looking our way while hanging out with cameras and lights.

"Hi, again," Kelsey says. She looks me right in the eyes, without the look of fear.

"Hi. How're you doing?" I ask. This hardly looks like the same girl who was frolicking on the beach without a care in the world. She is changed also with her distant, fiened smile and hard set eyes.

"I've been better," she says with an eye roll. "I hear you're having your face blurred out. So am I."

I feel a connection sitting by her. I knew there would be. We shared a tragic event, and we relive it repeatedly.

"Is your family here?"

"No," I answer. "I told them not to come. I just want to clear the record and start over somewhere else."

"I feel the same way; this money will come in handy." I don't see anyone around her; she is also here alone. She has been alone this entire time. I look around the large room. There are three large cameras on wheels, spotlights that are all off now, and those other people, who are milling about, whispering quietly. I'm not even sure where all this will be broadcast to, and the knot in my stomach squeezes tighter. Mandy appears and explains the process. Now that I see her in person, she is not how I pictured. She is probably five feet six and thin. Her hair is shoulder length, brown, and straight. I pictured a much taller girl, with big hair. She smiles with bright white teeth and red lips; she smells like cinnamon-apple. Her dress is very form-fitting, with black and purple swirls all around.

"Hi, Paul and Kelsey. We'll soon be sitting over in those chairs on the set." She points. "Both of your faces will be blurred out during the interview. Just answer the questions the best you can. The public wants to hear your story. It may get difficult, but just do your best. You will be paid by Randy after. I need each of you to sign this form. It is a waiver of liability or a disclaimer, if you will, to protect all parties." She points to Randy and to where we sign. We both sign. She gets right down to business. "Do you have any questions?"

We look at each other and shake our heads "No." Kelsey's face has healed up. As we move to the fancy chairs on the set, I ask her, "Where are you from?"

"Reedsville, a small town on the Ohio River." That is all she offers. I can see some perspiration on her skin. If I could, I would be sweating too. I feel some dampness on my back. I ask for some water first. Cindy brings me a glass. The people in the room become quiet, and the spotlights flip on. Two of the cameras get a little closer, and some men in suits remain standing off to the side. The lights are then dimmed some, and I see Mandy has a woman brushing stuff on her face now.

My chair is some sort of tan suede. How many people have been here, sitting on these chairs, telling their stories? I am starting to wonder if I'm doing the right thing. Will this even help people understand, or will they feel pity for me? *Just get it done. Picture a new place with new friends and new hobbies.* Hopefully, my grandparents will welcome me. I picture my new palm tree and me holding a new drink. I wonder if Kelsey would want to go sit and talk somewhere after this. We will have some money in our pockets, and I can find out what she's doing next. I wonder where she's going. Maybe back to Reedsville. The lights are strong, and they emit a dry heat. Will I even have time to talk to Kelsey after this? Will she even want to? I hope our bond doesn't end here. I want Kelsey, of all people, to understand, even if no one else does. I look at her; she looks very nervous now, like she is also rethinking this. Remember what Bonnie said: "You're a good person, so go tell your story." *Just get it done; get the money, and possibly get her phone number. You can do this, Paul.*

"Paul, are you ready?" Mandy is sitting on the other side of Kelsey. I nod. A guy in shorts comes over and places little microphones on us. A cameraman holds up his fingers to count down.

"Good morning. This is Mandy Brown, and I am here with Paul Duram and Kelsey Raymond. They are going to tell us the facts that led to the amazing story of actually saving the damsel in distress. At Bayliner's Resort here at Myrtle Beach, we had a fascinating story of a girl who was nearly killed and the stranger who saved her. I want to introduce you to my guests." The camera moves slightly. I fold my hands in my lap, remembering that my face is concealed; that helps. "Kelsey and Paul, welcome to the show." We both say, "Hello."

Mandy continues, "Paul saved Kelsey just in time, and in such a strange circumstance. We are going to ask just how this happened." Mandy turns toward us more now. "Kelsey, first, how did you know this man you were with?"

"We worked together and recently started dating, so this was just a fun weekend trip."

"So you had just recently started dating this man, and you went away with him to a hotel room?" Kelsey is rolling her hands in her lap. She clears her throat.

"We have been together for a while now."

"Did you even know anything about his past before you decided to go on this trip? Is this how you normally get to know the men you date?" Mandy waits for an answer. That question seems a little harsh. Kelsey stammers some.

"He was a really nice guy."

"So what happened that day to change this nice guy into a potential killer?"

"We went out to dinner, and we got into a fight."

"Was this the first time you had a fight with him?"

"Yes, I believe so."

"What were you fighting about?"

"He had some drinks, and he was flirting with another girl at the bar."

"So Adam, who was the new boyfriend, began flirting with another girl."

"It wasn't that recent," Kelsey replies.

I can tell this is not the line of questioning Kelsey was ready for. Now she is glancing at me with concern on her face.

"In the meantime, Paul, what were you doing during this time?" I am drawing a blank as to how to explain my behavior.

"Well … I … am afraid to say, I was hiding under their bed."

"So Paul, let me get this straight. You were hiding under these people's bed — people you did not even know. Were you going to surprise them at some point?"

"No, I was just wanting to experience other people's lives is the best I can explain it."

"So you are a bit of a peeping Tom in that you will break into people's rooms and invade their privacy."

"What you all can't see is that I am disfigured, and this was the first time I did anything like this. I wanted to feel part of a normal relationship, if you can understand that at all."

"How do you know what 'normal' is, Paul? Maybe most people are acting normal around you. Maybe you tell everyone this as an excuse to be a pervert and hide under beds." I picture my previous friends at Papi's seeing this and hating me. Mandy goes back to Kelsey.

"Kelsey, you were back in your hotel room arguing, right? Did you have any idea there was a person under your bed?"

"No, of course not."

"Tell us what happened next." Mandy is looking at Kelsey. I see all the people in the room staring at us; they are silent. Why did I think this would be helpful? I feel even worse.

"I was trying to leave, and he wouldn't let me."

"I understand this man was very muscular. Did it ever occur to you that being with an almost complete stranger could be dangerous? Did you ever think to get to know someone more before going away with them?"

Kelsey does not answer. I feel the need to help her out.

"I could tell she was trying to remain calm and not get him mad," I interjected. Mandy looks at me.

"How were you feeling about the situation, Paul? Did you at some point think to get out from under the bed before it turned violent?"

That's it — I'm done. This is not an interview but an interrogation. I stand up and rip the microphone off and storm across the set. I fast-walk right by Randy and head for my car. This is not the way I saw this interview going in my head. I wanted people to understand, not be on a talk-show parade of Mandy's pretentious questions. Now I feel like a pitiful ogre. I make my way through the hallways of previous arrogant news anchors and burst through the door, focusing only on my car and my escape from this horrible turn of events.

"Wait, wait!"

I turn around, and Kelsey is running toward me. "Can I go with you?" I process her request and open the passenger door as she flies in. She has a backpack with her. I guess she wouldn't have her bloody bag anymore.

"Where is your car?" I ask.

"I don't have one."

"Where do you want me to take you?" I ask as I pull away.

"I don't have any place to go." Kelsey has tears in her eyes. "Most everything at my place belongs to my friend, and I don't want anything reminding me of that day."

"Where are your parents?" I pull the car over at the bottom of the hill and put it in park to look at her.

"I can't go home. We don't really get along. It would be better for me to be homeless than go home. Can I stay with you for a little while? I don't have much money, either."

I don't understand what I am hearing. This girl is just a lost soul; sometimes I forget how many people actually have it worse than I do.

"Well, I was just about to head to Florida … today … actually … but I don't have much money, either." *I can't bring this girl with me to my grandparents' place; she is technically a stranger. My money will not last long.* Then I have a crazy thought. I put the car in drive and head toward my trailer, because I need my one remaining friend. We drive in silence, and she doesn't even ask where we are going. This girl trusts too many people. Soon I drive over the Waccamaw Bridge; I thought this would not ever happen again. I pull into Bonnie's spot this time and get out of the car. She opens the door and notices a girl inside.

"Is the interview over?"

"We left during the interview because it was more like a judge-and-jury show."

"Is that the girl?"

I nod "Yes."

"I'll take you with us. You said you have some money saved up, and we're nearly broke."

She smiles.

"Let me pack my bag, and we'll have to stop at the bank." Bonnie turns around and heads toward her bedroom. Kelsey gets out of the car.

"Who is that?"

"That's my neighbor; she is going with us to wherever." My mind is swirling. I wanted "real life" to happen to me, and I think it finally has. I can hear Mandy asking me this question: "Paul, when you were in the car with two people you hardly knew, what were you thinking?" I smile to myself. *"I guess I was happy not to be alone, Mandy, you bitch from hell."* Kelsey and I sit down on Bonnie's chairs to wait. She sits with me without any looks of unease or anxiety. A refreshing aura surrounds my soul. People are with me because they want to be; I turn my head so that my good side shows. I look over at my trailer and secretly take a picture of it. This is a memory I may want someday. Living here was the start of my independence and, from this point on, hopefully, my liberation. I remember the shark lamp I left on the side table. I still don't want it, because my new chapter is far beyond making a shark lamp.

Bonnie comes out with a medium-sized suitcase. We put it in the back seat with her. Kelsey keeps her backpack with her in front. She has even less than I do. Goodbye, Myrtle Beach.

M Y NEW LIFE STORY IS now going to begin, with Kelsey
and Bonnie in my car. I am elated to be sharing space
with people who want to be with me. These people chose to be
with me. My story could have started with plunging a knife
into a murderer's neck, but I would rather start it here. No
burns, no murder, and no wormholes, just a road trip.

We pull up to Bonnie's bank. She slowly waddles in. Kelsey
and I sit quietly. By the time she gets back to the car, she is
winded and coughing. I'm guessing she used to smoke. We
stare at her in silence.

"Don't worry — this is normal. Let's go, kids." She coughs
some more.

"South, right?" I ask.

"Absolutely. Are we going to the Keys?" Kelsey asks. I don't
plan on taking these strangers to my grandparents. My mom
would be furious. Anyway, the less Mom knows, the better,

right now. I probably need to call her before she has a stroke or something.

"Not right now. Let's get on Highway 17, and we'll get a map at the next gas-station stop." It will be my first map. I am not even sure how to read them, but Bonnie will know, I assume. I am sure I have navigation on my phone, but I've never used it. I followed Mom down here when I moved and have not gone anywhere since. Kelsey doesn't seem to have a phone, and Bonnie — well, I have no idea if she has one, either. I turn on the radio.

"What does everyone like to listen to?"

"Makes no difference to me," Bonnie wheezes out.

"Anything but rap," Kelsey says. I find a station playing old Rock and leave it there. Driving on the highway and heading for a new life. It's hard to focus with this unexpected company. I feel truly connected for the first time in what seems like years. When was I this happy last? I don't care about the interview or the lack of a job due to creepiness, because I saved this girl's life, and that's all that matters.

Driving across an overpass overlooking several train tracks outside of Charleston reminds me of a memory. I grew up outside of Ann Arbor. We lived in the country. Before the burn, I can faintly remember playing outside with my sister. We loved to explore. There was an old set of train tracks about a half mile away no longer in use, and we would play around an old, abandoned train-station building that was still standing. Nowadays, kids would not be allowed to wander off so far away. Tammy watched after me. She played hide-and-seek with me; I can remember hiding in the same spot several times. Maybe

I thought it would throw her off, but it never did. I had a hard time finding her. There were lots of trees and shacks around. One time she told me she was talking to a man who drove the train. She said he had on a gray suit with a whistle in his hand. He took off his hat to talk to her and told her when the train was leaving. I realized later she was not talking about a real person, but she wouldn't talk about it again. I wonder if she has ever had any other sightings like that. After my burn happened, all of the attention was on me. We never talked about the train man again. I thought about that man while I was recovering. I wanted to go and meet him myself, but I was hardly ever allowed to go outside for fear of infection.

I don't remember Tammy being around much after that. I just have memories of bandages and books. Mom spent a lot of time with me, entertaining me, teaching me to read and count. Did Tammy go out to the train station by herself? Maybe she did remember him, but she wanted to keep him all to herself. Did he become her new playmate while I was stuck in bed?

Once, when I managed to sneak out to find worms after a rain, I tried to hide them under Tammy's bed so I would not get caught with them. I remember all of the wooden crosses lying in straight lines under her bed. I decided my worms would not like the crosses because they would think they were in a maze, so I didn't want to leave them there. I never even thought about why she had those under her bed. I was so selfish and thought everything was about me. She never liked going to funeral homes or cemeteries. I figured that was because of Dad. Now that I think about it, Mom and Dad had crosses hanging in their room, and I don't remember him ever going to church. Mom would make Tammy and me go on occasion. Tammy would sit very still. I can see her face sitting in the pew. She appeared almost paralyzed during the service. I thought she felt bad for people staring at me, but no one was staring at me; the church people were used to me. I sang in the choir sometimes and took up collection. Everyone was nice. Tammy would not participate or speak. Why? I feel my hands getting tight on the steering wheel. The train man was very real to her. I was there, and there was no man there that day. Can my sister see ghosts or spirits or something? What was happening to her while I was taking up Mom's time?

Beth told me one time that she saw a ghost at the foot of her bed at her grandmother's house. We were all sitting around at Papi's late one night, talking about dying or something. Beth wore crystals around her neck with her long, black hair. I believed her story; she is too hostile to make stuff up. Brandon, my old boss, said his new wife had an experience with a ghost. In their house, growing up, she would see a woman in a dresser mirror. That was the only place, in the mirror. They just got rid of the dresser, and the vision was never seen again. Mirrors. There were no mirrors in my house ... I felt a palpable shift in my psyche; my childhood reverses in my mind. Bonnie speaks and breaks my spell.

"Kelsey, tell us some more about where you're from. Where are your parents?" A hesitation is noted.

"Well, my mother died last year. We lived in a small town on the Ohio River. Not much to do but watch the barges go by and pick tomatoes. Mom had cancer. It started in her ovary or cervix, something. She didn't like to go to doctors. By the time they found it, she lived only a few weeks. I never knew my father."

"Don't you have other family?" Bonnie asks.

"Well, Mom said they were all good for nothing, so I never really met them. I just decided to leave that small town and find a job. That's when I met Adam. Not a very good start out on my own." She starts to sound sad. I try to help the conversation.

"I left home a couple years ago, and I obviously made some bad choices, too, but it led me here," I say to her. "I'm glad I was there to help you. We both just need to get past this part of our lives. How about we find a place in Georgia to stay for a while?"

"My husband was from Georgia," Bonnie mentions. "I think he still has a sister there. I haven't heard from her since the funeral, nine years ago, but we could look her up."

"Doesn't sound like you were that close," I say. Bonnie coughs some more.

"She was an old hag then, anyway."

We drive past Charleston, almost to the border, before stopping for a break. We all get sandwiches, and I get a milk-shake with mine. They get Coke and some bottled waters. I fill the tank and walk in to buy a Georgia map. Bonnie pays for all of it. Same stares, like always. Silence befalls the checkout counter while the freak is there. But this time I'm not alone; I have friends in my car with me. I am king of the world today.

"Look how the people stare at you," Kelsey mentions. I look at her with an eye roll and shrug. We continue driving and eating. Soon we see signs that say we're approaching Savannah.

"I would love to see Savannah," Bonnie says. "I've been there once before, and it was magical. The moss-covered trees and beautiful architecture. My husband took me there for one of our anniversaries. We stayed in a bed-and-breakfast close to the Mercer House. I got to see the famous cemetery; you know — from the book."

I don't know what she is taking about, but I think of my sister again. "I would love to visit Savannah again, but it would cost too much to stay there or anywhere along the beach, for that matter." Kelsey is looking at the map.

"Hey, how about this state park not far from here? They may have those little cabins to stay in. It's called Gordonia-Alatamaha State Park." Kelsey can follow a map.

"As long as there aren't any woodpeckers, fine with me," I reply. A famous Savannah cemetery; cemeteries are strange to me. Growing up, I never saw them; it was almost like we avoided them. Once I drove by a cemetery close to the airport south of Myrtle Beach and had to stop. It was such a foreign sight, almost alien. All of those square rocks sticking out of the ground in order. Some were shaped like rockets. I remember standing among the stones after Dad took his life. Never since.

"I have to be honest about something," Bonnie says. "I told you my daughter is in Minnesota with her kids and husband. That is just what I tell myself. I have no idea where she is. Like my son, she could be dead for all I know. My grandkids are in foster care, and I will never see them again. I guess I should have been more loving and understanding instead of criticizing. Paul, you're not the only one who's made bad decisions.

I regret not having my grandkids, but I can hardly take care of myself."

I don't even know what to say. Bonnie and Kelsey both seem to have hard lives. I'd better call my mother.

After a little more than an hour, we arrive at the state park. I drive to the office, and Bonnie and I get out. Kelsey stays in the car. We go in and ask about cabins for rent. A nice woman named Angel helps us.

"We have eight cottages, and they are all furnished, with two bedrooms. Only three are rented now, so there's plenty of room. Here is the layout." She shows us a map of the campground, and we pick the cottage on the end by the lake. Bonnie gives her cash and pays for two nights. She starts coughing again while walking back to the car. Then I see her tissue, and it has some blood on it.

"Are you bleeding?"

"Sometimes I cough so hard, I get a little blood — nothing to worry about. Been like that for a long time."

I wonder how sick she is. Is she dying? Should someone know where she is? We get back in the car and creep along to the cottage. It looks like a little brown house and almost bigger than my trailer was. There is a little porch on the front. We all get out, and Kelsey takes a big stretch. She seems in a good mood. There are some folks fishing around the lake. I notice the quietness right away; peaceful. This will do for a while.

"I'll get your bag, Bonnie," I say as I lift it. She must not have wanted any of her furniture, either. Kelsey wins the prize for the smallest bag. Her life fits into a backpack; she must not have had a chance to shop yet. We unlock the door and go inside. It smells a little stuffy. Bonnie opens some windows. The kitchen is small, but it's still huge to me. The beds are small; I volunteer to sleep on the couch. I find extra sheets in a closet and lay them out for later. The walls are similar to Mom's storage shed but the furnishings are cute and homey.

I get some of my things out of the car and go into the bathroom when they are done. When I shut the door, I am reminded of being in that hotel bathroom with Kelsey just outside. I put that vision out of my head. I get out my lotion and hydrate my dry, molten-textured hide. I look in the mirror at myself. Could anyone actually love this? Mirrors? There were no mirrors in our house growing up. I thought it was because of me; what if it wasn't me? What if I am finally seeing life from other people's point of view? I have been so consumed by my own needs, I didn't look beyond myself. Dad didn't look into mirrors or go to church, so maybe he saw ghosts too. Is that why he killed himself? I didn't believe Mom when she told me it wasn't because of me. I assumed everything was about me. My whole life, I have been only thinking of me. I would hear about people's problems at work, but I didn't feel involved. Now I am in the middle of these other people's lives, and they do affect me. I'm finally considering problems beyond my own. *Paul, you need to open your eyes. Get out of your selfish wormhole, and see what's in front of you.*

I am thankful that Kelsey and Bonnie treat me like a regular person. Even Angel behind the desk seemed totally cool with me when we arrived here. *Not everyone is staring at you, Paul. The world is not spinning for you, and the sun does not rise and set because you exist. Call your mom,* my inner voice yells.

"The fridge is on. We should get some food," I hear Kelsey say through the door.

"You and Paul can go get some; I need to rest. I'll give you some money."

"That's awesome, Bonnie, thanks." Then I hear a door open and shut. When I come out of the bathroom, Kelsey is smiling at me. Bonnie must be lying down in her room.

"This is beautiful here, Paul. Thank you for letting me come with you today. I don't know where I would have gone."

"You know, I feel bad about not getting the money from the interview, but that lady made us both sound bad. I had to leave."

"A juicy story is better than a savior story," she replies.

"I guess I just didn't see myself looking any better after the interview. I hope you can understand my being under the bed that day. My life is rather boring and lonely."

"I might not understand, but you're forgiven, of course." She touches my arm while she says that. "Let's go get some food."

"Okay. We passed a Walmart close to here." I decide to text my mom for now and tell her I'm on a little road trip and will call her later. At Walmart, we grab some fruit, cereal, ham and cheese, milk, pop, nuts, bread, eggs, bacon, and chips.

After we get back to the cabin, Kelsey says she is going to take a walk. I can tell she wants to be by herself. She didn't talk much in the car. Bonnie comes out to the kitchen and gets herself a handful of peanuts.

"Kelsey is taking a walk." I can tell Bonnie is looking around for her.

"Do you know much about this girl, Paul? She sure is alone in this world."

"Her mom died, and she never knew her father. I'm guessing she's an only child. I don't think she has anyone else. I think this was meant to be. Do you have anyone we need to call?"

"Don't turn this to me. Do you realize she doesn't even have a phone? You don't find that odd?"

Bonnie seems suspicious of Kelsey for some reason. I thought about that, and I had noticed that she didn't have a phone.

"Maybe it got messed up along with all the stuff in her bag from the hotel. She just didn't want the phone back, either. The police may have taken it."

"She's still dealing with nearly being killed."

"We're all like a group of gypsies running from our lives," I reply. Bonnie laughs a little, which turns into coughing again.

"You kids will need to decide where you are going next, because I think that, after this place, I need to get settled somewhere. I have money from my husband's retirement and social security to live out my days somewhere I truly love."

"Bonnie, do you think we should try to find your daughter?"

"My daughter has been out of my life for years. She doesn't want me; I don't know if she's even alive. I couldn't control either one of my kids. They both ..." She shakes her head.

"I'm sorry." I don't know what else to say. I'm not used to consoling someone else and hearing other people's problems. The world is so much bigger when you take an active part in it.

"I won't bother you for long. I'm just glad to be somewhere else. Perhaps we can find a nice retirement community somewhere, and you can drop me off." Bonnie has her eyes closed again.

"Sure." Is that what she really wants? I have no idea.

"I just want to live my life till it's my time." She smiles. I look toward the door, wondering where Kelsey has gone to.

"I'm going to go outside for a while. Are you okay?"

She nods. "Paul, have you told your family where you are?"

"I do need to call Mom. I also feel the need to call my sister, Tammy. She lives one town over from Mom. Howell, Michigan, and I think I may owe her an apology. I am realizing my life was not quite how it seemed growing up." I walk out and look around. I don't see Kelsey anywhere. I look at my phone. No service. I'll have to call Mom later.

I walk toward the lake. I have seen some beautiful lakes growing up in Michigan, but this is just as nice as any. I soon find Kelsey sitting along the edge, looking straight ahead.

"Would you like some company?" I ask.

"Sure. It's beautiful here. I could live here forever."

"Well, perhaps you can. You can get a job here and mow grass or work at the office or ..."

She hits me in the ribs.

"You're so funny. I've never met anyone quite like you. You're a little crazy, but in a good way, fun way. I never thought I would be hanging around with that person under the bed, oooohhhhhh," she says with a scary voice. "I understand why you did it. I can see how some people react to you."

"Thanks for understanding. I'm really not a pervert, just curious, more than anything."

"I'm glad I have this chance to get to know you," she smiles.

I turn to the water, trying to remain cool. This beautiful girl is enjoying my company; my heart is jumping out of my chest. She is sitting by my good side now, so I will stay facing the lake. If only I could cover up the rest of me.

BONNIE GIVES US SOME money to get dinner together and bring back food. The evening is chilly, and Kelsey seems to own only a few summer dresses and flip-flops. We go to the local bar for dinner; I like dark tables in the back because fewer people notice me that way. We get some glances as we go in. I need to realize it might be because of her, not me. She is stunning, with her hair a mess and light-blue dress. She does not wear much makeup, maybe some lip stuff. I face the back wall when we sit down in the booth, and she faces the bar. I notice she looks at the crowd often instead of me; probably doesn't want to stare. Maybe she just enjoys looking around; it might not be about me.

We have a nice dinner, and I talk about working at Papi's. I will miss my friends there. I already feel like those days were a long time ago, not just a week ago. Kelsey does not give much information. I wonder if she is ashamed or just private.

"It is getting colder outside. Do you have any warmer clothes to wear?"

She turns to me and shakes her head "No" with a small grin.

"We can find a Walmart to get some more food and you some warmer clothes if you want. I can pay for the clothes."

"That would be great. Thank you, Paul," she says as she looks down. She must be ashamed.

"Do you have any money?"

She faces the patrons again and shakes her head "No." *She was doing the interview for the money, just like me.* Now she has nothing. "Do you know what you're going to do?" She continues to shake her head without looking at me. I think tears are forming in her eyes.

"It's okay, Kelsey. Everything will turn out fine. I'll help you. Bonnie seems to want to help us both out." I touch her arm, and she doesn't pull away. *Is this the first time I have touched someone other than family?* I pull back before it does get weird.

"Thank you. I don't know where I'd be right now."

"Where were you living before the …" I express with my hands.

"I was with a girlfriend, but it wasn't really working out. I wanted to get my own place but could never save up enough money. Then *he* wanted me to pay for some of the vacation, so there went what savings I had. I should have seen him for what he really was." I look over toward the bar to see what she's looking at. She touches my arm this time.

"I'm sorry. I just feel bad not paying my share," she explains.

"I won't charge much interest," I smile. She giggles. We finish eating and drive to the Walmart. I am shopping again with someone other than Mom; what a wild experience. *Paul, play it cool.* We get some more chips. Kelsey wants some Coke, and I get Bonnie some cough drops. She picks out a couple sweatshirts, black tights, and socks. I make her pick out a pair of shoes. We don't go to the underwear/bra area. She also buys a travel bag and some shampoo. While we check ourselves out, I hear someone snickering. We look over, and a couple guys buying beer are looking at us. I continue bagging, and Kelsey stares at them until they quit looking at us and get on their way. We drive back to the cabin after grabbing Bonnie a fish sandwich and fries.

"Do you ever get beat up?" she asks.

"No, I didn't go to public school, for one, and moving to Myrtle Beach was the first time I ever really experienced life. Being exposed to people made me curious to be around people more, so that's when I decided on my little game. You were actually the second time I did it. I can't believe I'm telling you this," I confess. "And hanging around with you and Bonnie is very new to me. I feel like a different person, and I'm learning more about myself, my childhood, and I feel more aware. That is all because of you and Bonnie. All of my life, I have felt like family are the only ones who would ever be accepting."

"What did you do for work?"

"I washed dishes. I could tolerate the hot water on my numb hands and was used to being alone. The job just fit me, but now I may want more for myself."

"Where did you want to go next?"

"I really don't know — just enjoying this for now. I know I don't miss living in that trailer all alone."

She looks straight ahead while I talk and drive. "I saw some bikes under a shelter behind the camp office. Do you want to go for a ride tomorrow?"

"Sure," she answers.

Bonnie wakes up from watching TV on the couch when we enter; she eats her food and goes to bed. It's been a very busy day, so Kelsey decides to go to bed too. I make up the couch with the sheets and use the bathroom when it is free. I wonder if the rooms have locks on the doors. Does Kelsey wonder if I will sneak in and hide in her room? Does she even think about me at all? I don't know how old she is, but I don't really care. It's sad that she doesn't have any family; are *we* like a family? Do strangers just meet up and roam the earth together all the time? I have no idea. Is this normal? Is there any part of my life that has been normal? Crap, I forgot to call Mom.

I see Tammy at the front door to our old house. She is like a zombie. She is standing outside the door, and then she rushes just inside the door; she waits a few seconds and rushes back outside the door. She repeats this over and over. I can't get her to see me or stop. I run to find Dad. He is at the back door, and he's doing the same thing. Inside, outside, inside, outside. He doesn't see me. I run through the house, yelling for Mom. I find her upstairs in the bed. I tell her to come downstairs to help them, and she tells me, "No." I beg her, and she looks me in the eyes and says we can't help them. Mom tells me that Dad and Tammy are see-ers, and see-ers cannot be helped. I squat down to hide under Mom's bed. More crosses.

I wake up to light coming through the windows. My dream is still in my head, and so real. I don't remember that happening, but it did seem real. A cold chill runs down my spine. I decide I'd better call Mom today. I leave a note and drive my car three miles to town, to where I have phone service. She answers right away.

"Paul, I've been worried sick. Where are you?"

"I'm at a state park in Georgia, staying in a cabin."

There is a short pause, and her breathing is audible.

"Okay, what is going on with the incident? Last I heard, you had to wait to be cleared."

"It is all done, Mom. I'm cleared and free to go. I couldn't stay there anymore."

"Where are you going? Do you want me to come down now?"

"No, Mom. I can handle it."

"But you have been through something traumatic, and I don't want you to be alone."

"Well ... I'm not alone ..."

"Who are you with?"

Why do I feel like I need to keep this a secret? I'm not doing anything wrong.

"I am with a lady who was my neighbor and the girl I saved at the hotel."

"Paul, what are you talking about? Why are these people with you?" She's getting upset.

"Mom, the three of us all needed to get away, and we are having a good time." She is silent.

"Well, can I have their names?" she asks calmly. "I would like to know who you are having fun with."

"Kelsey Raymond and Bonnie … I guess I don't know her last name. I have known her ever since I lived at the trailer. I think she might be sick, because I have seen her cough up blood. She can't walk very far without getting out of breath."

"Is she smoking around you?"

"No, she doesn't smoke, Mom."

"And that girl, doesn't she have a family?"

"Apparently not. She was alone and was still living at the hotel. We'll all be going our separate ways soon. I know it seems weird, but it's good."

"That girl sounds like trouble," she remarks.

"She just needs some help for a while. She was there with me, Mom, and it was not a good experience. I feel we're meant to have this time together to heal and … get beyond it …"

"Where are you going next? My parents were wondering if you are going down to see them."

"Probably soon, when I'm alone. Okay?"

"I will text you their address in Florida. Let me know where you are every day, please. I hope you get down there soon."

"Hey, Mom, how are Tammy and Jamie?"

"They're fine. She thinks Johnny might pop the question this Christmas. I think they are finally ready to get married, for goodness sake. Jamie is so grown up."

"What has taken them so long to get married? I don't think I ever knew why they haven't yet."

"Tammy never wanted to," she explains briefly. "She has always liked her own space."

I contemplate that for a moment. *Her own space. What does she need space from?* Quiet job, one easy kid, doesn't live with Mom. Very interesting.

"Mom, I'm going to go now. I'm good, and I've got money till I find my next job," I declare.

"Well … thanks for finally calling me … and I love you … I can come down anytime, you know …"

"Love you too. Bye." I hang up. That's done.

I go back to the cabin. I smell bacon. Bonnie is up cooking.

"We don't have any coffee, and I need coffee," she says.

"How do you take it? I will go get you some."

"I like some creamer. I don't know if Kelsey likes coffee."

"I will just get her one of those long-named fancy drinks. Be right back." I'll get a fancy drink too. Why not? The McDonald's right beside Walmart is bustling. I'm anxious to see Kelsey this morning. After our dinner last night, I want to spend more time with her.

I finally arrive back, and Bonnie happily takes her cup; Kelsey is still not up. I knock on her door quietly. I hear her mumble.

"Got you a frappé coco latté fufu out here if you want it." I hear growling. She opens the door, grabs it with a "Thank you," and goes back to bed with a shut of the door.

"Guess she's not a morning person," Bonnie mentions.

"Guess not."

"Do you like scrambled?"

"My favorite."

She whips them up in a bowl with a spoon, just like Mom did. I am ravenous. The drink isn't too bad, either, but I usually just drink water. Grew up that way to keep hydrated. That was Mom's favorite word — hydrated, hydrated.

Bonnie and I decide to sit by the lake after breakfast. I carry the chairs over. It is cool enough to need a sweatshirt. Bonnie has a jacket on that looks very old. It might actually have a picture of a cat on it.

"Do you like cats? I am surprised you don't have one for company."

"I did till last year, but she got old and took off one day. She left me to die, I figured. Headed for the marsh. Everyone tends to leave — the cycle of my life."

I don't know what to say, so I say nothing.

I'm faced with more turmoil from others. Is this how Mom feels? Dad left her, and then Tammy, and I don't want her to help me now. I thought I was just giving her a break from me. Maybe moms don't want breaks. After Dad took his life, the house fell silent. I was old enough to realize what happened. I still don't remember what Tammy was doing. How can I be so selfish? She lost Dad too. I remember my wounds were all healed up, and Mom let me go outside more often. After I finished my schoolwork, I wanted to escape the house. I would run and climb and dig, but Tammy and I hardly played outside together anymore. On rainy days, I remember playing with Legos. I was not very good at building them. The pieces were too small for me to grasp. Mom got me the big, fat Legos, but I thought they were for babies. I liked to spy. I remember walking in the woods behind people's homes and listening to them having cookouts or jumping on trampolines. More memories are coming back to me. I forgot about spying on neighbors; I was trying to be a part of others' lives even back then. I would be gone for long periods of time on my adventures. What was I escaping? Tension. I seem to remember tension. Tammy never smiled, did she? What was she doing? When I got older, I fell into the video-game world and hardly ever went outside or noticed anyone else.

Tammy did not do well in school. Her grades were mostly Cs. I would get jealous because she went to school and got poor grades while I was stuck at home. I would sometimes be pissed at her for having a place to go; it was always about me. She dressed in dark clothes for a while. She and Mom would fight occasionally. I didn't pay any attention to what they were fighting about.

"Paul, Paul. Did you have any pets?" Bonnie startles me.

"No. Mom didn't want to risk an infection. When I got older, I guess nobody wanted a pet." *Is that true? Is that why?*

"I don't have a cell phone. I just had a landline in the trailer. I was wondering if you could search on your phone for an assisted-living facility around Savannah, Georgia, and call them. Find one where they have some activities. I'd also like a pool; I think that would help out my joints. The thought of spending the rest of my life there sounds perfect."

"That sounds good. I'll make some calls later, when I can get service. Kelsey and I are going for a bike ride today. We'll ride into town, and I will do some searching for you."

"Thanks," she says. The cool wind starts to blow, and she coughs. It takes a while for her to catch her breath. Then she sounds like a rattle for a bit.

"Can I get you anything?" I ask. She shakes her head and puts her hand on my arm, while coughing again. We sit and watch the water ripple in the wind for a while. She heads back to the cabin. It takes her a long time to walk back. Mom would know what to do if she were here. I think about Tammy again. Mom was taking nursing classes while I was hooked on Halo. Tammy finished high school and moved out. I think she lived with friends till she got her own place. She sure wanted out of our house. Eighteen, and then she was gone. I feel very selfish. It took a life-changing event in my life to open my eyes.

Kelsey comes out to the lake with her new sweatshirt and tights on. She has on her new tennis shoes. Her hair is all rolled up on top of her head. She sits in the chair Bonnie was in.

"I don't usually get up this early."

"What shift did you work?"

"I went in around twelve and left around seven. They liked having someone there late to take calls. Perfect for me."

"I used to work from three to eleven. I didn't stay out late after work."

"Why?"

"I don't know — nothing to do," I admit.

"Are we still going for a bike ride?"

"Yes. I need to put my phone on the charger for a while first. Be right back." I hop up and go to the cabin. I plug my phone in. Bonnie walks out of the bathroom; she looks annoyed. She looks out the window and then looks at me.

"Kelsey didn't even say 'Good morning' to me after I greeted her. Is she acting okay?"

"Seems to be. Maybe she didn't hear you. I see her staring at nothing sometimes. I think she's still traumatized."

"You can make excuses for her all you want, but that girl is trouble. What do you even know about her? Because she doesn't share much with us." Bonnie sounds like my mom.

KELSEY TELLS ME THAT she'll get a new phone when she's settled in a new town. She doesn't have anyone to call, anyway. This girl is a lost soul. She is nearly killed by her boyfriend, abandoned by her father, mom dead, and living with people she hardly knows. She is too trusting. We are like each other in the ways of the world. Internally alone and dealing with the struggles life has handed us. She's abandoned by family, while I'm abandoned by society. I think she has accepted my blunder — the under-the-bed incident. There is no judgment or blame or questions. Too bad she couldn't live on "misfit island"; she is way too beautiful. If Kelsey was in my life, however, I wouldn't need "misfit island."

The beauty and the beast; is that relationship even possible? Her judgment might be clouded with the fact that I saved her life, but she is still here. She's comfortable with me. I'm still coming to terms with the fact that she's here. One day, I'll wake up, and she'll be gone. Kelsey will realize she doesn't have to be here with us, but she is. My heart feels like it has grown in size. I picture her sitting at the table with Mom, Tammy, Jamie, and Johnny. We are having a big dinner, celebrating my sister's marriage. Kelsey mentions how she loves my family, and they find her delightful. An actual girlfriend for poor Paul. I need to stop this. I'm getting ahead of myself. *Just focus on your next move: helping Bonnie out and trying not to fall in love.*

Kelsey likes to spend time by herself. I can't push her to find out what she's thinking; she's still dealing with trauma. I need to be supportive and show her I can be patient. I am also coming into a realization in my own life. My life growing up was not quite how I thought it was. How do I just now realize that? Dad and Tammy had a secret. They did not want to share this secret, at least not with me. I even remember Dad wanting to move away from that house, but he took his life before that happened. They saw the dead. Tammy saw a dead train engineer. There were crosses all over the house. There were no mirrors. Dad did not kill himself because of my trauma, and Tammy did not disappear from herself because of me. Does Mom know all of this? Why did nobody tell me? Books. Were there books about this kind of stuff at the house? I don't remember any, but I did not look, either. I don't even remember where my sister was most of the time, let alone what she was reading.

I am a little ashamed for not knowing what was going on around me. A selfish boy living in his unfortunate body. Now is my chance to help others and to make a difference. *You were put on this earth to accomplish something; it is time to find out what.*

After a lunch of cold cuts and chips, Kelsey and I decide to go for our bike ride into town. The sun is up, and it's warm, but I still cover most of my skin. She wears one of her dresses with the black tights and flip flops. I guess it's just a leisurely ride. I grab some cash and my phone, and I put a pen and paper in my pocket to write down information for Bonnie. We go to the office and pay the twenty-dollar rental fee. Neither of us has ridden in years, but it feels great. Kelsey looks like a princess, with the wind blowing her long, brown hair and a smile on her face. This seems like a great idea for healing mental wounds. My face will look like a crazy blur to most people going by, so this makes me feel almost normal. When I get settled into my new place, a bike will be my first big purchase. I hope Kelsey and I will be riding together.

When we get to town, my phone lights up. Missed calls from Mom, Grandma Jean, and another number. We pull over by the little grocery store. I tell her I need to check on some things for Bonnie. She says she will ride around some more and come back. I listen to the voicemails. Mom just asks me to check in, Grandma wonders where I am headed to, and the mystery number is Officer Corbin, wanting me to call him back. I instantly feel sick; what does he want with me? I text Mom and Grandma, telling them I think we're headed to Savannah, Georgia, for some sightseeing. I call Officer Corbin back, and he answers on the fifth ring.

"This is Paul Duram, returning your call." I try to sound unconcerned.

"Hi, Paul. How're you? Ya staying out of trouble?" He actually sounds very cool.

"Yes, doing fine."

"Glad to hear it. I'm just calling to see how you're getting along." *Wow — that's a relief.*

"Actually, I am with Kelsey now. We kinda left town together for a fresh start." I don't hear any reply on the other end of the line.

"Paul, are you serious? That really doesn't look good. I would almost think you two planned the murder together if you weren't such a dumb kid to just tell me that."

"Oh — I never thought of that. We were just doing that interview together I told you about, and we decided to abandon that idea. Please tell me you didn't see us on TV."

"I don't know anything about your interview, but I find this news a little troubling. I don't want to hear any more stories about you."

"You won't," I tell him firmly. "Well, we're also with my neighbor. It is a long story; we're just chilling for a while."

"Just take care of yourself. Goodbye, Paul. If you need anything, give me a call."

"Thanks. I will, sir." He hangs up. That was nice of him to check on me. I never thought of the fact that people would think Kelsey and I planned that whole thing. I wonder if she has thought of that. I look around for her — nothing. Is it not logical that we are getting to know each other after that event? I notice the sign for the grocery store, "Reidsville Market." I just remembered that was the town Kelsey said she grew up in. Funny coincidence. I wonder if she noticed that? I won't ask, because it sounds like her childhood was not too good.

Hard to believe she has no one out there who even knows she was almost killed. I would be lost without my family.

I decide to do some research for Bonnie on old-people homes in Savannah. We drove around Savannah on the way here, just about an hour back. It looked like a busy town, older, no skyscrapers. What are they called … assisted-living homes? There are several, so I call the first three to find out if they have rooms. Two of them did. I don't write anything down, because it looks like we will be able to find her a spot. I see carriage rides are available in Savannah. It does look like a magical place. Maybe I will want to stay there; I like big old homes. I could work in a kitchen. Kelsey could work there too. Bonnie would love that. Then I won't feel like I am leaving her in one of those places. We would be much happier there than the trailer park. Maybe there is a doctor on-site who can check out her cough.

I sit by a tree in the shade, waiting for Kelsey to come back. There is a bar across the street. Cute place. I get the idea to ask Kelsey out for dinner tonight, only this time it's a date. Do I dare? I don't want to scare her off by being forward. I need to find out what she likes; I don't feel like I know her. Did she go to college? Who is her best friend? What's her favorite color?

I want to talk to her without the thought of her looking at my scars. If I could just cover myself up. I could wear bandages on myself except for my right eye and right side of my head. I will look like a mummy or something. I go into a store two buildings down from the grocery. It has used clothes, shoes, and some furniture. I find some scarves. There is a black one, and I could tie it around my face. This would look even worse, like some sort of cartoon character. Then I find a black hat and black button-down shirt. If they were all together, perhaps it would work. I buy them all. The woman at the counter does not say a word to me. She fumbles with the items putting them into a bag and charges me less than what was on the tags.

"Thank you," I say.

"Yes, thank you," she replies. Then she fumbles again while I take the bag. I see Kelsey once I'm outside. She's waiting by my bike and doesn't ask what I have. She looks happy.

"Are you ready to head back?" I ask. "Or are you hungry?"

"We can go back. Did you find out the stuff for Bonnie?"

"Yeah. We're going to go back toward Savannah probably tomorrow and check it out. How does that sound to you?"

"Sounds good."

"Kelsey, do you know what you want to do next? I'm just wondering." She is quiet. "I don't mean to pry or anything."

"I know. I'm enjoying myself. If it's okay, I would like to stay with you for a while."

I am overjoyed to hear that. She wants to stay.

"Can you see yourself in one of those big plantation houses, working for someone? I could try to find some work in a restaurant." I wait for her reaction. Nothing. We get on our bikes and start back toward the park. The wind is blowing her hair again. She smiles at me and then finally answers.

"I can see myself waiting tables or walking dogs for some old ladies." We laugh at that. "Let's take another road to make the ride a little longer." We turn left onto Hill Street and make a right on Smith Avenue. We come upon a cemetery. It's big and partially surrounded by an iron fence. The sign says "Reidsville Cemetery."

"Is that the name of the town you were from?" I ask. She looks at me and hesitates to react. Then she smiles.

"Wow — good memory, Paul." I like the way she says my name. She looks back toward the gate. I think of my sister. She would never have stopped in front of a cemetery. She would be looking the other way and holding her breath till we were well beyond it. Tammy held so much mystery inside of her. I feel like a failure of a brother now. She was close to Dad, and I was close to Mom, till Dad was gone. Then Tammy was close to what, who? I feel the need to get off the bike and walk toward the bench outside the iron fence. I wonder if I can channel my inner soul; maybe I could see or feel a spirit of some kind. I sit down and close my eyes. I realize I do hear something familiar, a woodpecker. Behind the cemetery is a line of trees, and the sound comes from that direction.

I realize that Kelsey is sitting by me now. She is quiet. I open my eyes, and she is looking away.

"Kelsey, what's your favorite color?"

"Ummmm … I would have to say lavender."

"Do you believe in ghosts?" She turns toward me with a mystified expression.

"I didn't see that question coming," she laughs. "I guess there might be. I never had any kind of experience. Why? Have you seen them?"

"No, not me, but I think my sister sees them."

"Cool. When I was young, my mother thought I was possessed by some sort of spirit. I guess I started dancing erratically for days. I was told I had tarantism."

"What is that?"

"There are two theories, really. One is an uncontrolled nervous impulse, like hysteria, and another is a person is bitten by a tarantula, so you have to dance off the spider venom. We lived in Louisiana at the time, so either theory is possible. Like I said, my childhood wasn't the best. I was young and feral." I don't know how to respond to that. It doesn't sound like anything I ever heard of.

"Do you hear the woodpecker?" She nods. "Did you know the black box inside of an airplane is protected in the same way a woodpecker's brain is? They also made helmets based off the way a woodpecker's brain is protected from the pounding."

"Are you a bird expert or something?"

"No, just woodpeckers." I smile. She looks toward the trees.

"That's cool about your sister. Are you trying to see a ghost here?"

"Well, I was thinking about it. I wonder if genetics might play a part in seeing ghosts, because I think my father could see them too. Let me get a picture of us both with the cemetery in the background, and then I can check the picture later on for ghosts." I hold my camera out.

"No, no. I don't like my picture taken." She jumps up and startles me.

"Sorry. I didn't mean anything by it," I stammer.

"I know. I just don't like …"

"No problem, I'll just take some of the cemetery."

Kelsey walks in the other direction while I take some shots. Maybe visions will show up in the photographs. I close my eyes and think about that train engineer. Is he still there, walking the tracks every day? Did Tammy ever see him again? The thought gives me the creeps. The few hairs I have on my torso are on the back of my neck, and they are standing up. I am suddenly parched. Parched from the exertion of biking or parched from spiritual beings around us — I don't know for sure.

"Are you ready?" she hollers. I nod. We continue on this road, which takes us back to the main road, Highway 30. She sure was weird about the picture thing. Maybe I should be with family instead of wandering the earth with people I don't even know. *Paul, what are you doing? Hanging out with a girl who was nearly killed and possibly bitten by a tarantula and your neighbor possibly near death herself. You have family who love you and a sister you need to reconnect with. Wake up. Go home. Face the consequences of your actions, and quit running away.* I'm not running away. I'm riding bikes with a beautiful girl who enjoys spending time with me. What could be better than that? Right. Right now, nothing. My bag is flopping around my wrist as I ride. Life is good.

The bikes are ours all day. We ride back to the cabin. The sun is getting hot. I go in and drink my fair share of water and sneak into the bathroom to apply my lotion. While my shirt is off, I try on my new black shirt and hat. They all smell clean, good enough. I try to tie the scarf just right to hide most of my face, but it keeps falling off or moving over my good eye.

My handsome eye, the eye that shows the world what I could have been, but nobody notices that eye.

"Are you okay in there? I hear you banging around," Bonnie says.

"I'm okay." Maybe she can help me with this thing. I open the door, and she looks at me. Then she smiles, because she knows just what I am trying to do so badly. She pushes her rather large self in with me and shuts the door. She takes off the hat and scarf. She holds it up and folds it over again; then she places it across my face. It is more stable now; she ties it behind my head and then puts the hat on, tilted back some, so some of the light shows off my good eye. It stays in place.

"That looks great. You feel the need to hide yourself?"

"I just wanted to see what I could look like." She walks out and sits on the couch. I can hear her whistling deep breaths. I fear she might be getting worse, but I don't say anything. She will be seen by someone soon.

"I called some places for you, and there are openings. There were plenty of them to choose from; thought we would head there tomorrow."

"Sounds good. Living in Savannah will be like a dream. I'll take a shuttle into the downtown area every day and find the perfect bench, under the perfect tree, with the perfect drink, and soak in the culture," she replies.

The TV here is always on some cooking or remodeling show. *She'll need a TV in her new place, Kelsey will get a new phone, and I will get a new life.* No more hiding out in the back of rooms or kitchens. Maybe getting caught under a bed was the best thing that could have happened to me. I wonder where

Kelsey is. I check myself out in the mirror one last time. Such an altered appearance that I hardly recognize myself. This will be so much fun to pull off. I change back to my regular clothes. I walk outside and see her on a chair beside the lake. I grab some more water and a chair to join her. When I sit down, I realize how tired my legs are, and achy. I am more out of shape than I thought. Now is the time to ask her out on a real date. I want her to know how I feel. She is drinking a Coke and eating some chips.

"This is a nice place. I was thinking about dinner tonight." I stagger a little, and she interrupts.

"I'm going to go into town again on the bike. I enjoyed the ride, and I want to pick up a few more things I need. Then I'll grab a bite to eat while I think about my next move."

"Do you want to use my car?"

"No, I enjoyed the ride. Very freeing, and it got my mind off my recent situation."

"Oh, okay. Sure." I did not get to ask, but I did get another idea.

"Did you see any spirits in your pictures?"

"I haven't looked yet. It's too bright here to see right now." We enjoy the heat and breeze together. Being here with Kelsey is as good as being at any beach, but then she gets up and heads to the cabin.

"See ya later," she calls.

"Yep," I reply. I look down at my hands; I need gloves to cover them up too.

14

LATER THAT DAY, I see her leave on her bike. She changed her clothes. Her hair is pulled up, and she has on a different dress, blue, with her black tights and a sweatshirt tied around her waist. She has her backpack on, which is practical so she can put things in it that she buys. I wave to her, and she waves back with a smile. By now, I have moved under a tree. My sore legs don't want to move. She must be in much better shape than me. I'll have to work on that. I head back to the cabin since she's gone. Bonnie is asleep, sitting up, facing the TV.

I decide to look for gloves first. I open drawers in the cabin — none. I try the bedrooms, looking for anything. I see a screwdriver in Kelsey's room. It is sitting on the dresser beside a broken outlet cover. How strange to see this again; a screwdriver in a bedroom. I suddenly sense the fluid running down my hand; only my mind feels the warmth. This screwdriver has a flat head; the other one had the star pattern. It was another lifetime ago when that happened, to a different guy: a guy who was always alone, a guy who was self-absorbed, and a guy that never saved anybody. Not quite a hero, but I am the dishwasher who saved a life. Perhaps in a terribly bizarre way, but it still counts. I continue looking for gloves. I remember I have big yellow ones in my car from work that I never needed. Those would look stupid with the black clothes. I will just have to keep my hands down.

I'm going to go to that bar across from the grocery, and I'm sure Kelsey will eventually go in there to get a bite to eat. It looked like a fun place. I will surprise her with my altered appearance. Walk right up to her and ask to sit with her like I don't even know her. I laugh inside at my idea. We can talk more about our childhoods and our crazy lives. She can look at me, focusing on the good eye without trying to look through a horror show. Hope the people at the restaurant won't think I'm going to whip out a gun and rob them, with my half-covered-up appearance.

I drive into town around four-thirty and figure I will arrive before her and get all set up at a table. Looking at myself in the mirror, with my new black shirt and hat on and my scarf ready to slide on, I feel good. Have I ever felt that way looking at myself before? When she comes into the bar, I'll be there to greet her like a rogue stranger. I park in the back to hide the car a little. I see the bike parked beside the grocery store as I walk around to the front. I don't cover my face yet, but I do pull the hat down some. Just as I enter the door and turn the corner, I see Kelsey, already sitting at the bar. She is talking to a man. They are very close together and very close to me, so I quietly step back behind the corner again. I hear her giggling. That familiar girl-giggling, and I'm suddenly back in my wormhole spying on strangers. Of course, she would be talking to someone; she's a hot girl who appears to be alone. She came in to relax, and any man would want to talk to her. My plan is not starting out quite like I pictured, and then I hear them talking.

"I can't believe you're just passing through and you stopped here," the man says.

"Why can't you believe that, Bill? I bet you meet up with all kinds of girls passing through." I hear her voice, and it's different. She has a smooth, sexy way of talking to this man. I can almost feel her pressing herself right into him.

"Never anybody like you," he replies with vigor. "What are you going to do when you get to your brother's house?"

"Find a place to live and get a job. I just hope it all works out." A hint of desire mixed with seduction and full-out lies. "I think it's so cool that you are a ... what is it?" She giggles some more.

"A surveyor. I verify property lines using special equipment. Every time property sells, I locate property markers for the landowners. It pays well, and there is a wad of cash just burning a hole in my pocket," he brags. "There are times when I could use an extra set of hands. Maybe you could stay around for a while. This town is friendly, and people mind their own business." Now he is totally sucked in.

"Are you asking me to stay here with you?" she says, real slow. "I took a bus here just to rest for a while and never

thought I would run into someone like you in this little town."
More giggling.

"It must have been fate. Let me get you another drink.
Are you hungry yet?"

"Yes. How about a burger and fries? Do you like a girl
with a good appetite, Bill?"

I can't believe her voice. Not at all the shy, innocent girl
I have known for almost a week now. This girl is completely
different. Then, I realize that I have been spotted.

"Sir, do you want a table?" a waitress asks me. I stay close
to the door.

"No, I am waiting for someone first," I say in a low tone.
She looks at me with caution and then walks away. I continue
listening.

"What about your brother?"

"He'll be glad I'm not coming. He's got a new girlfriend
and probably wants to be alone, anyway. Do you know what I
mean?" Kelsey speaks with that country drawl. She was never
planning on staying with us. She was planning to ditch us.
I have heard enough of her poor-girl routine, so I walk out
and head for my car. I tear off the hat and scarf and throw
them on the ground. Once in the car, I'm furious. She is just
trying to get away from me. Liar. I am sick at myself for being
such a stupid idiot. How could I think she would be interested
in someone like me? She was just using us for a temporary
escape, till she found something else. I make myself calm
down before I drive.

I start the car and head back to the cabin to think of my
next move. *Okay, Paul. You will never get to sleep tonight, and*

*you are supposed to take Bonnie to Savannah tomorrow —
remember?* I will need a little drink tonight to get my mind
off this whole situation and help me sleep. I turn back around
and stop at the grocery store. There are a few select bottles of
booze in the back; I grab one, not knowing how it will taste.
A tall man is at the cash register. I pay while the man checking me out wants to see my ID. I hand it over, and he asks if
I am new in town.

"No. Been here for years. Just got out of my bubble," I say.
He does not talk anymore. I leave with my brown paper bag.
I want to go back into the bar and confront her, but I decide
it isn't worth the scene. Then I arrive back to the cabin and
realize I forgot to bring Bonnie back any food.

"What happened?" she asks. She can see that I am alone
and very upset.

"Sorry, I forgot to get you anything."

"I can make some eggs — no problem. What happened?"

"Let's just say it will just be me and you tomorrow." I go
into the bedroom that Kelsey was using and close the door.
I open the bottle and take a big swig. Melky Miller American
Whiskey, the bottle says, and it tastes terrible. It burns and
makes me want to puke, but I don't care. I see a few things left
on the floor that are hers from the Walmart: a dress, a hair
tie, and the tennis shoes, which I knew she did not like. She
probably never planned on coming back when she left. Well,
this is my bed tonight, and she can have the couch if she happens to show up.

I take a couple more swigs to make sure I go to sleep.
I strip down to my shorts. I don't feel anything yet. A couple

more swigs. I miss my family. My mom was right. She was concerned and had every right to be. I am traveling with a sick, elderly woman and a girl who is just using me. What am I doing here? Now I suddenly miss my simple life. My beach, job, and those videos served me just fine. Now everything is messed up. I will always be the guy from under the bed. I know a tear is running down the right side of my face. The room is suddenly spinning now. I hold my head and turn to face the cheap little dresser and stare at it with the light coming through the little window. It's too early to go to sleep, but I don't care. Tomorrow I'll help Bonnie find a nice place and then head for my grandparents in the Keys; I can always count on my family. I lie back on the bed. It smells like her. It smells so good, which makes me all the madder. She sure fooled me. No regard for others. I miss Taylor; she was a good friend, and look what I did to her. She may have gotten into trouble with me stealing her key card. She never did text me back, and that breaks my heart.

I hope Kelsey does come back, just so she can sleep on the couch, and I can leave without her tomorrow. I remember my sister sleeping on the couch. She dressed in black clothes most of her high school days. I thought she slept on the couch so she could sneak out of the house, but I don't remember her ever doing that. She would tell me it is too "busy" upstairs in her bedroom. I never cared to think about what she was talking about. She wanted to tell me, but I wasn't listening. Dad killed himself upstairs. My poor sister, tormented and alone. Tammy had this whole other life, and I had no idea ... spinning ... room.

I am suddenly awakened by a knocking on my door. I look around the now-dark room and see the time is ten after two. It is Kelsey, pounding lightly.

"Paul, are you in there? Sorry I'm so late, Paul."

I can tell she's standing there, waiting for me to answer. I will savor this moment for a while. I know the door is not locked, and I don't respond. She finally opens it, and I sit up. "Oh, I guess you're sleeping here tonight?" she asks.

"Why, yes, I'm sleeping here tonight. The couch is too lumpy."

"I'd feel much better sleeping here. Could we switch? 'Cause all my stuff is in here."

"Take your stuff with you." I lie back down and pull the blankets up. She does not move or talk, so I'm guessing she now knows something has changed between us. I can't wait to leave her in the morning. I guess it didn't work out with the mystery guy. A smile is on my face as I fade back to sleep.

MY EYES OPEN BECAUSE I smell smoke. I can hear crackling sounds. I bolt upright and look around. The clock now says four thirty-six. I can definitely smell smoke. I stand up. The room is no longer spinning, and as I look out the window, flames are dancing all around. I quickly slip on my jeans and grab for the door. The knob turns, but the door is jammed. I yell.

"Kelsey, Bonnie — open the door!" I pound on the door with both of my fists. I listen — nothing. I turn the knob again, and the door will not pull in. I shake and kick the door with all of my might. "Kelsey, Bonnie, get up! Open my door!" I hear nothing but the crackles of flames. The door is not hot, so the fire must just be outside. The light does turn on, and I slip on my shoes so I can kick the door harder. I kick with all my might, which must not be very good. Panic sets in. Where is everybody at? I grab the knob and try it over and over. The door will only move less than an inch, because something is catching it on the other side, and it is not going to open. I scream more times, yelling for help. I turn around to the little window. Flames are completely covering it now. I put on my shirt and my jacket and zip it up, because this is where I will have to get out. I hit the small window several times with my fist, and the glass does not break. I look at my hand, and it is turning red from the heat and hurting from the pounding. *Oh, my God — what is happening?* I run to the bathroom and turn on the shower to drench myself quickly. Then I face the window again; the wall is getting hot, and I need to get out.

Looking around for something to break the window, I see the screwdriver on the dresser. I grab it and stab the window with it. Flames are climbing in toward me. I use the screwdriver to break out all the glass by running it along the edges because I will need all of this space to get through as fast as possible. I grab the bed and drag it to the window. I pull my wet hood up over my head, step on the bed, and throw myself through the flames feet first, holding onto the top frame of the window with my sleeves pulled up. It takes a few seconds to maneuver myself through and, once I touch the ground, I fall and roll to make sure I'm not on fire. I look at the cabin, and it is engulfed. I run around to the front and I hear sirens in the distance. My car is gone. Standing here alone, I try to contemplate what is happening.

I need to see if anyone is inside. The front porch is burning up. I run through it and try to open the door — locked. The floor might collapse under my feet. My wet clothes and feet are not on fire, but I am feeling heat through my pants. I step back off the porch. I get a few breaths of clean air and decide there is no choice but to knock this door down. I run back through and, using my momentum, it busts the door open. I enter and see an empty couch. Some light comes through the front door from the security lights outside. My bedroom door has a chair under the knob, so it couldn't pull in and the table is jammed into the chair. Bonnie just has a chair holding her door shut. I hold my breath and run for Bonnie's room. I pull the chair out of the way and go inside.

The smoke is thick, and the light switch does not work now. I can hear faint coughing. I find her on the floor covered in a blanket. The heat is intense in this room. I tell her to get up, but she just coughs. I grab her under her armpits with my forearms and, with great effort, start to drag her out of the room toward the front door. I keep the blanket on her. She is breathing in the toxic air, and her coughing sounds high-pitched.

"Hold your breath, Bonnie!" I yell while I breathe in the smoke. She is very heavy for me to drag. When I am almost to the front door, three firemen bust in, and all grab ahold of her and carry her out. I run through the flames one last time and fall on the ground, gasping. When I can finally breathe again, I look down at my hands. They are black. I can't tell if they are dirty or burned. I reach for my face, and everything feels normal. Then I start to feel my legs. The backs of my legs are burning. They hurt because the backs of my legs were not burned in my chili accident. Then one of the firemen is beside me and tells me to breathe in this oxygen. He puts a mask over my face, and I just lie there. I turn my head over toward the fire truck and read the words on it: "Reidsville Fire and Rescue."

I wake up to a familiar smell — a hospital smell. I look down at the bandages. My hands, arms, and legs are wrapped up. My eyes are burning, and my head is wrapped up. I am immediately thrown back to being four years old and looking at all the bandages, lying on the hard plastic bed with prison rails up, yet this time it is just side rails, and I am alone. The freak is all alone this time. The freak who made the bad choices. The freak burned again. My eyes start to focus and tear up; the burning is all too real. I look around the empty room. Then I think of Kelsey. She did this. She took my car and started the fire. Where is Bonnie? Is she okay? I push the button for the nurse using my whole hand. A black man comes in, wearing green scrubs; he has a big smile with very white teeth.

"Hey there, Paul. I'm Samuel. I'm your nurse aide and your official bandage wrapper. You have been on some pain medication while we cleaned you up. I've never seen such a thing. We couldn't figure out your skin till we talked to your mother."

"How did you talk to my mom?" I asked.

"Your cell phone was in your back pocket. It's right here. Amazing that it survived the fire." I look over and see it. My only possession now. Samuel starts taking my temperature and blood pressure.

"How is Bonnie?"

"Well, I don't know about that, buddy, but I will let the police know you can talk now. They have been waiting to talk to you. Oh, and your mother is on her way here. I'm sure she will be here sometime today, because we talked to her yesterday morning." Samuel sits down and holds a glass of water with a straw for me. I empty the glass. Now I notice that I have an IV hooked up to my right shoulder. That brings back more memories. I have so many questions. I need to talk to Officer Corbin now.

"Samuel, can you scroll through my call history for me and find a number that is not with a name?"

"Sure." He quickly finds the first number that is not recognized and reads it to me.

"That's it. Press to call, and put it on speaker." He lays it down on my tray.

"I'm going to go make some calls now too. This is about to get interesting around here." He leaves.

"Hello. You have Corbin."

"Hey, this is Paul Duram."

"Hey, Paul, what's wrong?" He is surprised to hear from me.

"I need your help; you're not going to believe this story."

"With you, yes, I will believe it. You sound terrible. What's wrong?"

"Well, Kelsey and I got into a bit of a disagreement, and, then, in the middle of the night, the place we were staying in is engulfed in flames and she is gone along with my car. I don't even know if Bonnie, my neighbor, is alive." I feel the stress of all of this coming at me again, and the blubbering starts. *How could she do this to us? What kind of maniac tries to burn us alive?* I can no longer talk, and my body starts to shake. My face is trembling. Samuel walks back in and sees me in this pitiful state. He takes my phone and talks into it. My only function is to look toward the window and envision the flames outside.

The next time I am awake, it's dark outside. My mom is right by my side. I can see the tears in her eyes with the faint fluorescent lights overhead. They must have given me something to calm down. My limbs are all heavy.

"Just rest, honey. You need to heal up." She holds my bandaged hand, and we both cry. I know she is just glad I'm alive, and I'm just glad she's here. I manage a couple words.

"Is Bonnie alive?" She shakes her head. I close my eyes.

I am in my childhood bedroom. There are tracks all around the walls; train tracks go in and out of the room. Soon I can hear the train coming, and it's a pink metal train. Kelsey's face is the front part of the train, and she tries to run over me. Her train keeps coming at me from all directions to knock me down. I run to the bathroom and shut the door, but there are tracks going through the bathroom too. I wait to see which track the train is going to come at me from. I am so scared. I hear it coming. Kelsey laughs as she barely misses me. There is no escape, and the train gets faster and faster, zooming around the tiny room. Finally able to reach for the door, it opens, and I'm facing a wall of flames.

I wake up. I feel hot. My legs are hurting and burning. I reach for them. Mom is still beside me.

"Paul, you now have second-degree burns on the backs of your legs." That was one of the places I did not have burns before.

"What about the rest of me?"

"You have second-degree burns all over, but you can't feel a lot of it. It was smart of you to get all wet first, honey. That might have saved your life while you were climbing through the window."

"How did you know I climbed through a window?"

"There were other campers down from you, and they saw you come out the window and then crash through the front door. Paul, I hate to tell you this, but you are all over the news again. Man goes back into burning building to save elderly woman. You're a hero."

A hero. I was just trying to save my friend. Wow, it's my own personal 9/11. But she still died. She still didn't make it.

"But she died, Mom."

"But she didn't have to burn to death, and she was not alone. Her lungs could not handle all the smoke. She told the firemen to thank you." I see Bonnie in my mind. She did not deserve that ending. She just wanted to have her little piece of Savannah. I wish that she was still living in her little trailer and that I had never gone to get her. I can't believe the way my life has turned. I wonder where Kelsey is.

"Have they found Kelsey?" Mom shook her head, again. My legs hurt more. I try to move them.

"Do you want more pain medicine, honey? I'll go tell your nurse." She rushes out the door before I can even answer. I look over at the window, scared I will see fire again, but this time I see a bright blue sky. Mom comes back in.

"They want you to talk with the police before they medicate you again."

"That's fine. Will they be here soon?"

"Yes. Here, have some water." Just like old times. Water, water, water. I think about what I have left of my life. Nothing. Most of my stuff was in my car or burned in the cabin. *No, Paul. Don't feel sorry for yourself. A hero? Not hardly. I still feel like a freak.*

"I need to get up and pee, Mom," I realize. I sit at the side of the bed for a while and Mom puts my IV on a pole to roll around.

"How do you feel?"

"Not bad." I stand up while she has a hold on me, and we walk a few steps to the little bathroom. "I'm okay."

"Well, I'm right out here if you need anything." I stand in front of the toilet for a while before I can start going. I know there is a mirror right beside me, but I am afraid to look into it. What am I going to look like this time? I turn to face it. My skin has a red tint to it, but no blisters or skin sloughing off. My head is wrapped up for some reason. I take the wrap off. The hair on the right side of my head is still there. There is a gash on the left side of my head about three inches long, with white tape strips across it, which I do not remember getting. Not bad otherwise. I walk back out and Mom looks concerned, seeing my cut.

"How'd you do that?"

"I have no idea." I lie back down, and a police officer comes in.

"Hello, Paul. My name is Kevin Brown." He puts out his hand and shakes my bandaged hand carefully. He looks around fifty years old and tired. "I was hoping you felt up to talking to me about what happened. This has been a very interesting case, and when I talked to Officer Corbin on the phone, it got much more interesting. I'm so happy that you're doing this well after what you have been through."

"Thanks," I reply.

"Paul, I got a lot of information from Corbin about what happened with you and Kelsey in the hotel room, and now you were traveling together, along with your neighbor?" He seemed puzzled.

"I was all ready to leave town by myself when Kelsey suddenly wanted to go too. I thought, 'Great!' at the time, and my neighbor wanted to get away, and she was going to help with the expenses. She paid for the cabin rental and some of the food. I was going to help her find a place to live around Savannah. You know, like an old folks' home, because I am sure she had some health problems, but she wouldn't talk about it. Bonnie was always nice to me, and we were doing each other a favor." I can feel the emotion building. "I know it seems odd, but her kids aren't around."

"So tell me about Kelsey?"

"Everything was going great. We were all having a good time, an adventure. Then there was a problem." He looks at me, waiting patiently. I drink some water before telling the sordid details. "She took a bike into town to have some alone time, I guessed, and I was going to surprise her later on. When I found her, she was talking to some guy and being very flirty, and it sounded like she was going to stay with him. She talked about a brother she was on her way to stay with. I didn't know anything about a brother. So I went back to the cabin and had a few drinks, because I was upset that she was planning on ditching us."

"Did you like this girl?"

"I guess so, but not after I heard her with this other guy, so I took her room. I was surprised she even came back at all; she wanted her room back so she didn't have to sleep on the couch. I wouldn't give it to her. The next thing I knew, the place was on fire, my door was blocked with a chair, and my car was gone. She did this!"

"Paul, another party at the campground saw you climb out of your window, and then you went back in to save Bonnie. You had already suffered burns and trauma. I commend you on your bravery and sacrifice. Not many people would have done that. We are in the process of trying to find this Kelsey Raymond. We know that Bonnie's purse was taken, and you don't have a wallet. We have who we assume is Kelsey on camera pumping gas into containers using your car. Her face and hair are covered with a hoodie. We are actually having a hard time finding out anything else about her. We don't even know if that is her real name. After the incident in the hotel, the police didn't take any pictures or fingerprints of her because she was the victim. Now we realize we dropped the ball on that."

I still can't imagine her buying gas and starting that fire after stealing from the both of us. How can I be so blind and naïve to have let this stranger into my life? She seemed so nice. I remember Officer Corbin telling me about the circuit boards in Adam's bag. He was tampering with them to steal out of clients' homes. Did anyone think that Kelsey was doing this with him? It might have been her idea. Nobody pointed a finger at her, the poor-little-girl victim.

"Is there anything else you can think of to locate her?"

"I can't believe anything she said now."

"I am sure there will be more questions later on. Get some rest, and I'll see you soon. Sorry about all of this happening to you." He put his hand on my shoulder, one place without a bandage. Mom was standing quietly behind him the whole time. I'm sure she would like to say, "I told you so," but she doesn't say anything. Then Grandma and Grandpa Foraker come in, my mom's parents from the Keys.

"Hey, kid — you were supposed to come down and see us," Grandpa says while he bends over and kisses the top of my head. Grandma has tears in her eyes.

"I'm okay, Grandma. It looks worse than it is. I can't even feel most of it." She really cries now.

"Pauly." She always calls me "Pauly." "You are going to put us in an early grave."

"I'm sorry, Grandma."

"Have they found that girl yet? I just can't believe this!"

"No, I can't believe this happened, either." I am feeling tired and sore. I give Mom a look, and she knows just what to do.

"Mom, Dad, let's go get a bite and let Paul rest." The nurse comes in and gives me something in my IV. Mom ushers them out and slips back in to tell me my other grandparents wanted to come, but she told them to stay at the shop because I will get out of here soon. I take another drink and wonder about my sister. Did she want to come? Is she tired of poor, poor Paul getting all of the attention again? I wouldn't blame her. I'm sure that Jamie needs to be in school, and Tammy is busy. I feel the medicine working. My phone is sitting beside me, and I remember the pictures I took at the cemetery. I study them and turn them upside down, but I don't see any spirits or ghosts. I set my phone back down and think of the wood-peckers, with Bonnie and me sitting outside in the shade. My little boring trailer life sounds good right about now …

16

I WAKE WITH A CLEAR HEAD. Mom told me I am at Optim Medical Center and that they would release me tomorrow. She wants to take me home with her; sounds good to me. There is a text on my phone from my sister dated a couple days ago that I missed. Tammy says she loves me and hopes I can come home soon. I would like to get to know my sister better; it would be like starting at the beginning with her. I wonder if anyone got ahold of family for Bonnie. Did anyone even look for her lost daughter? Is Bonnie with her husband now? I now believe in spirits and ghosts, but I was not born with the ability to see them, like other members of my family. I would not have had to sneak under beds to get a thrill if I could see ghosts. My life would have been completely different, possibly worse. There are no wins to either situation.

Whose life is great? Nobody I know. People struggle with who they are and who they are with. A person does not really know what's around the corner. People leave, cheat, lie, and die. No control. Alone. I think of my "misfit island" dream. Could that work? A place where everyone has their own deformity or disability? It probably couldn't work, because they would fight among themselves about who has the worst problem or hardest life. What was I thinking? Yeah. *Join the real world, Paul.* You are now a part of it, and it's going to bite back. Remember, this is just what you wanted, to be included in real lives. No longer an outcast living along the edge of society; you have been pulled right in.

Officer Kevin Brown knocks at my door and walks in again.

"Hi, Paul, you look rested. Fewer bandages." I'm sure it was hard finding something nice to say while looking at me.

"I am better. Did you find her?" I'm anxious to know.

"No, we are running into dead ends. I did go and talk to her and Adam's previous employer at the security company. A couple of the employees said they thought the couple knew each other before Kelsey started working there. Kelsey may have even been hired on because Adam already worked there. Nobody had any pictures of her on their phones. Some had pictures of Adam. They said he was a good-looking guy who was into himself, with stuff like tanning, weights, and he was smart with computers. After he got hooked up with her, he was more distant and didn't go out with the other employees anymore. They had a hard time believing he could be violent, but it sounds like she could manipulate people. We just can't get a photo of her, and her prints are not in the system."

"You got her prints?"

"They were on the doorknobs — easy to get. You don't have prints, and we got Bonnie's prints after she passed. We know Kelsey and Adam both lived in Reidsville, North Carolina. She lived with a girl ..." My head snaps up. Reidsville again.

"You know what? She told me she grew up in a town by the river called Reedsville, in Ohio, and now you're telling me she lived in an apartment in Reidsville, and then she picked the place where we could stay for a while, which was Reidsville, Georgia. This can't be a coincidence." Kevin looks at me dumbfounded and takes some notes down in his little book. He looks puzzled.

"Maybe she plays a little game with herself, her psychotic trademark or something. She always stays in a 'Reidsville' somewhere," he concludes.

"Exactly!" I shout. Maybe now she could be found, if she stuck to her cycle.

"I'll try to locate some family back in Ohio, if she's really from there. She might even go home. Don't worry, Paul. We'll do our best to find her, but it'll be difficult without any pictures." I know what that means. With all of the crime that goes on, the effort to find this girl will be short-lived, because they don't have the manpower, and people are murdered every day. "Here's my card if you think of anything else." He stands. I take his card and tell him, "Thank you." I wonder how many states have a "Reidsville." I wonder what happened in Ohio to create this wicked girl.

"I do have another question before I go," Officer Kevin asks. "Did you know Kelsey before the hotel incident?"

"No," I say. "I thought you talked to Officer Corbin and found out the history."

"Yeah, I heard the story, but I just had some questions. You said there was a disagreement because of a man she was talking to at a bar, and then you took her bed. So she started a fire to kill both you and Bonnie because of a reassignment of beds?"

"I'm just as shocked as you."

"Well, just one more thing, Paul. We'd like you to stay here in the area after you're released from the hospital, until further notice. We just have some more things to clear up."

"Okay, sure," I stammer. He exits. I feel uneasy now, like I did something wrong. My head is spinning. *Do they think I was part of a big plan, a conspiracy to kill Adam?* Kelsey probably drove him to kill her. I place my head into my hands to think. What did Corbin tell the police here? Don't they believe me?

Mom comes back in next, with her parents. They all stare at me like strangers — or is that just my imagination? Samuel and Mom change my bandages together. All of the burns are just second degree or less, so no more permanent damage — not that it would have mattered. I'm healing up well, but my mind isn't on my skin. I'll get out of the hospital soon, and then what? I'm not even going to mention that I can't leave to Mom.

It's nice to see my other grandparents; I just wish it was down on the beach, like my original plan. My skin couldn't take any hot weather now, so I will gladly go home to Michigan with Mom. I just wish I knew when that could happen. I'm sure this is just a small formality, normal procedure, but I feel sick. I just want to find another job and get my own place, incognito again.

We all walk down to the cafeteria for lunch. It's the first time out of my hospital room in four days. My legs are sore, but much better. I just have to go slow. The pizza looks good, but I eat only a couple bites. I must have lost about ten pounds already. They all watch me look at my food. I look around to the people in the cafeteria, and some are looking at me too. *The freak is out!* Let them look, I don't care anymore. Life is not about me; life is a crazy, mysterious ride. We slowly walk back. Down my hallway, I see the back of a girl, and I immediately think of Kelsey: long, sandy-brown hair, thin, same height. I hold my breath partially out of fear, but, when she turns around, it's not her. I know Kelsey is long gone with my car and that my stuff has been dumped out somewhere, but she haunts me. She needs to be found; this girl is pure evil. I picture her driving in my car state to state with Bonnie's money.

"Hey, Mom. We need to call the insurance company and credit card company."

"Already did. Grandpa Ed did it for you. He said you used the same insurance as him. If your car is not returned by next week, they will be sending you a check. We can call your credit card when we get back to the room."

"I think we'll need to go shopping. I have no clothes."

"We will; there are a few things still at the house that you can wear," Mom says. "We'll get you all fixed up." Why did I ever leave Mom in the first place? Oh, yeah. To get my own life. Stupid.

I should tell Mom what the policeman said to me, but I just want to talk to Officer Corbin first. He'll get all of this straightened out.

By evening, Mom goes back to her hotel, which is just a few minutes away. I call Officer Corbin. He does not answer for once, which makes me all the more sick. I leave a message. I'm sure to be released by tomorrow. I take hardly any pain medicine now, and I can walk. My head is healing fine. I wonder what they did with Bonnie's body. I really can't worry about that now. I try to watch TV, but my mind is racing. Stay around longer … why? I'm just a dishwasher … just a stupid boy who met up with Miss Kelsey Raymond, a.k.a. your worst nightmare in a cute little package. She will latch onto anyone she can use, manipulate, and discard.

I remember her on the bed right after I killed her boyfriend. She was scrunched up to the top of the bed and hiding behind a pillow. She was barely making a sound and staring at me. I guess that was because she was actually scarier than anything else in the room. Scarier than the big man trying to kill her and scarier than the little freak who killed the big man. She was not even that upset about almost dying. No hysteria. No conscience — that's what it is: she's dead inside.

My phone rings and startles me. It's Officer Corbin, thank God.

"Hi, Paul. I thought you might be calling me."

"What's going on? This Kevin guy came back and asked me if I knew her before. Do they think Kelsey and I were in together on killing Adam?"

"Well, they do think the situation feels off. They wonder if she was getting rid of you because you knew too much and are a potential witness against her." I ponder that.

"I told them that I completely believed you the day Adam was killed, and I have a good gut instinct. But they don't care about my gut instinct, Paul, they want some hard evidence to prove you were not a part of this."

"What do I do?" I plead. "I can't believe this is happening."

"I also want to tell you that this Officer Kevin and his partner, 'Sheila,' or something, came up here. They searched your trailer and talked to people you work with." I'm going to be sick.

"I didn't do anything," I cry. "I can't face my family if this gets dragged out more."

"Paul, they also took your bloody clothes you had on that we had for evidence. They will be tested for carpet fibers since you said you crawled in and out from under the bed. Once they find the fibers, I'm sure you'll be cleared. They also checked your cell phone-activity; there was nothing suspicious."

"Okay, okay — that's good." There should be fibers. I did slide around on the floor a lot. "Do you think that's all they'll need?"

"She did have marks on her face from the pillow abrasions; the scene was just how you said. They just want to confirm your story."

"But I could have been under the bed waiting to kill him!"

"You stole the key card from your friend. We all know that. Don't worry. Nobody wants to pin this on you, Paul. You pulled your neighbor out of a burning building. You just had a run of bad luck is all."

"Corbin, I'm scared. What if she's never found?"

"I think you're safe."

"What if she wants to get rid of me because I know what she looks like? She wouldn't let me take any pictures of her. Now I know why."

"We'll find her. Don't worry. I gotta go, buddy. Hang in there for a while longer." *Click.*

But I'm a witness. When they find her, this will all go to trial, and she'll find a way to get rid of me. I stand up; I can't just lie here … I walk to the window and look down at the ground. Is she out there now? Maybe she never left, because she has unfinished business. I look all around at the trees, the cars, the signs, the bushes, and the people. Do the police realize I may be in danger, not an accomplice? There won't be any sleeping tonight.

B Y MORNING, I CONTEMPLATE that, when I am released,
I can't go home with Mom, and maybe I shouldn't
anyway. I need to continue with my own life, take care of
myself, and keep any danger away from my family. I'm sure
to be released from the hospital today, and I want to go back
to Savannah. It should be close enough to be in the area.
Bonnie made it sound very appealing. The haunting history
of Savannah intrigues me. If there is any chance of me seeing
ghosts, that would be the place to try. I want to step into famous
cemeteries and actually walk among some tombstones. I can
try to conjure up my own ghosts. I now know that Tammy and
Dad did not have good ghost experiences, but I still want to
be a part of their idiosyncrasy. There is no way Kelsey would
know where I was.

Breakfast comes in: folded eggs, toast, sausage, and juice.
I'm finally hungry and eat it all. Samuel finds me a couple

donuts. He leaves my bandages off today and takes out my IV. Mom arrives and puts on a brave face for me. She has some clothes in a bag.

"Has the doctor been in yet?"

"No. You should've seen me eat breakfast — I was starved." I still don't mention the restrictions and suspicions. I just hope for a miracle soon.

"Do you want me to get you anything else?" she asks.

"No, I'm good." Mom looks more rested today. Her parents must have left; I don't ask.

Kevin, the officer, calls my phone.

"Paul, we have some good news for you. Your car has been located at a bus station in Oklahoma. Your belongings are still in the trunk, and the car is being shipped here now. We will need it for a little while, and then it will be returned to you. We did find carpet fibers on your clothes from the hotel. Frankly, that story is too crazy to make up. You're free to go, unless you're going to wait for your car. We have also located the gentleman Kelsey talked with at the bar that night. His name is Bill Lehman." I'm all ears waiting to hear about this. "Bill states he was talking to her for quite a while. States she seemed desperate and had only a bag with her. He figured she was trouble, so he wasn't going to take her home with him."

I was confused. "They sure sounded like they were getting together," I argue.

Officer Kevin continues, "Bill stated she was beautiful and told her those things just to get a piece of … ass. He told her he couldn't even wait to get her home, and they got busy in the parking lot. Then he left her there. Part of her anger

OUT OF THE WORMHOLE

toward you may have been because of what happened at the bar. She got tricked and took some of that anger out on you, which makes the fire more believable."

"Wow." Another crazy encounter of lies and deception.

"We also located Kelsey's mom. They were, indeed, from Reedsville, Ohio, with two 'e's.' Her mom now lives in Glouster, Ohio."

"Kelsey told me her mom died of cancer."

"Nope, her mother admitted that Kelsey was her daughter and that she escaped Kelsey as soon as she turned eighteen. Peggy Raymond is her name. Peggy and Kelsey did not get along, and Peggy was scared of her own daughter. We even contacted some of their old neighbors and were told that Kelsey was verbally and physically abusive to her mother. Peggy admits to leaving one night and not telling Kelsey where she was going. They'd been renting an apartment. She didn't care what happened to her daughter, but she was certain Kelsey would con or steal her way through life."

"Does she have any pictures?"

"We asked her that, and no. Kelsey had destroyed anything of value to her mother: pictures, keepsakes, and any maternal feelings." He is wrapping this conversation up. "We'll still be in touch, and you've got my number. Again, you are cleared. All of the evidence points to Kelsey. Have a good day."

"Bye." Mom waits for me to explain. I share with her the crazy details about Kelsey.

"Honey, I can't take much more. Please, keep your life simple from now on, will you?"

"I promise, Mom — I want simple too. I just want to ask you something." She sits down on the bed beside me. "Do you know anything about Tammy and Dad seeing ghosts?" She looks surprised by my question.

"Well, yes, Paul. They do — or did — have that ability. It caused some problems in the house." I wait for more details from her this time. She fusses with her hands. "Your dad would see things at the house, so we were getting ready to move, hoping that would help. Your sister started talking about things she saw too. I tried not to make it a big deal, because I didn't want to scare Tammy with this ability that she had at such a young age. I didn't know what to do with either one of them. I took care of you, because that's what I could do. Your dad had some intense visions … and …"

"Is that why he killed himself?"

"Yes, honey. He just couldn't take it, I guess. He didn't tell me about everything that was happening to him; he started to withdraw. I knew the spirits he saw were not always nice. Sometimes he would leave for days, because he would get in trouble at work with his behavior, so he would just sleep in the car at work and not come home. After he ended it, I didn't have the motivation to move. Tammy started seeing more visions, and they were not always at the house. I figured it wouldn't matter where we lived. When she got older, she slept downstairs; she seemed better if she avoided the upstairs."

"Why didn't anyone tell me this stuff?"

"You had your own problems, honey. I was just glad you didn't also inherit their abilities."

"I thought Dad killed himself because of the way I looked all these years."

"Oh, honey, no. Your dad loved you very much. He was just suffering from his own demons."

"Did you know this about him when you two met?" She pauses to answer me.

"I did, but back then, his visions were nice, and we had fun with it. But, at some point, they turned more sinister." I think about all of this, and my fascination about the other world is even greater. How could all of this have been happening right under my nose? All that I thought about the world has shifted to a new dynamic. Between Dad and Tammy's ability and the evilness that is out there, my concept of the real world is forever altered.

"Mom, I'm not going home with you, because I want to continue on my own. All of this must be happening to me for a reason, and I have to go find my own way." She holds my hand.

"Okay. Well, then, Mr. Grown-up. Where are you going to go?"

"Savannah, once I get my car. I'll get one of those cheap Airbnb places till then." I couldn't stay in another hotel or cabin right now.

"Do you want me to stay with you till you get your car?"

"I know you need to get back to work, Mom. I'm okay. Kelsey sounds like she has taken off far away, and she won't find me. I'm used to being alone — remember? And right now, that's what I crave. No offense." I pull on a smile. Dr. Cook walks in to see me.

"Good morning, Paul. You're looking well today."

"I feel good." He looks me over for a while.

"I'm going to release you now. Can you please avoid anything hot?"

"Sure. No problem, Doc."

He's gone again. Mom sits down in a chair; she looks like she's a million miles away. I google Airbnbs here in the area to stay at till I can get my car. I find some whole houses and some couches. No, thanks. Then I run across a bedroom in a place run by an older couple. Perfect. It's walking distance from a couple restaurants. It's close to here, in a town called Claxton. I book it with Mom's credit card.

"Can you spot me some money till I can pay you back?" I ask, and Mom smiles.

"No more traveling with strangers, right?"

"Promise."

Samuel comes in with the discharge papers. I wait in a wheelchair till Mom pulls up. We go to an ATM and to a small grocery store in Claxton for some snacks. We find the little house, and she insists on coming in with me to see it. The owners are there and greet us without stares or comments about me. They tell me how to get into the house. Mom picked up some clothes for me yesterday. That will get me by till my car is returned with the rest of my things.

We stare at each other once I'm settled in. The room has a clean smell, and the hosts don't ask questions; they're very nice. This will work for a few days.

"I just want to rest now. You go on home. Thank you for everything. Sorry you've had to deal with so much between Dad and me. I'm sorry."

"Don't you worry about that. Just let me have some peace for a couple years, okay?"

"Sure."

She hugs me goodbye, and I fall onto the bed. She has a long drive home. I wish I was going with her, but I need to find my own way. I thought I was tired, but I'm hungry again.

18

THIS BED IS GREAT, and this room is quiet. It's been two days, and I'm waiting to hear about my car. I use money only to eat and take walks frequently to get my strength back up. The nice lady let me eat cereal yesterday morning, and, today, she had warm blueberry muffins. I'm paid up till tomorrow with Mom's credit card. My skin is healing up. On the outside, I'm back to my same ol' frightening self, but on the inside, I'm a changed person. There is a darkness channeling me, and I'm wondering if I now have more abilities like Dad and Tammy. I was not looking for this altered self, but it chose me; I feel a difference. If people stare at me while I'm on my walks, I stare right back and hold my gaze, daring them to say something. The expression on my face is harder, urgent. I feel a sharper intensity. No more hiding in the light. Here I am — deal with it.

As I walk past the tire store again, I get a feeling in my gut. I smell the familiar rubber, and the tire-changer tool makes me jump every time. My intuition tells me there is something I'm missing. I think about what Officer Kevin told me about Kelsey's mom. Kelsey is a violent con and sounds like a psychopath. Maybe she drove Adam to the point of wanting to kill her, but then it hits me. I freeze in my tracks. What if he wasn't killing her? What if it was a game they were playing — a sex game with play-acting?

Watching them on the beach, I never saw any hint of fighting; it was always very sexual, but Kelsey has an obvious fondness for violence. Maybe she got him to play this little game before sex to heighten the pleasure. It might have all been an act. He was never going to actually kill her — she just liked it rough. But he put marks on her face! Was that all the more fun for her? I'm standing like a statue on the sidewalk. Cars are going by, but they no longer register. Clouds are overhead, but are they actually moving? I don't know anymore. Reality has been altered again for me. Did I kill an innocent man? Is that the real reason Kelsey did not seem so scared? It could have been because she is a true psycho, but it also could be because he wasn't actually going to kill her. The element of surprise was *me* — not him. She didn't mention the possibility that they were playing a game to the police. Nothing was said. Why?

I guess it plays out better for her as a victim. She got special treatment from the hotel and didn't get questioned about playing a dangerous game. No pictures were taken of the poor victim. He was the one with the circuit boards, not her. She was just an innocent person, while he was stealing.

The circuit boards were probably her idea in the first place, and she just needed someone smart to pull it off. Adam was just another one of her little game pieces to use, according to her mother — her mother, who abandoned her one day and never looked back. Maybe Kelsey was planning on leaving him soon; he just didn't know it yet. Maybe she wanted to play the game to destroy him with physical evidence. My mind is spinning with all the possibilities. Do I call someone with this information? I might be wrong, but I have no idea. Does it matter now? I can't change anything. I continue walking to the house and straight past my hosts playing SKIPBO® again.

On my bed, I feel sick. I don't even know what to do now; another universal shift. This could cause trouble for me, if they somehow prove he was not really killing her. I can't tell anyone about this; it will have to stay with me and my new, dark existence. This guilt must not take over; I don't know anything for sure. *Paul, you don't know.* My skin suddenly feels tight and dry like a worm on hot concrete, far from the soft, moist dirt and far from any rescue.

My phone rings later that afternoon. It startles me out of my trance. It's Officer Kevin. I tell myself, *Talk normal, Paul.* He tells me I can get my car back now. It's at the police station in Statesboro, Georgia. That's where the area forensic department is, and they're expecting me. All I have managed to do this afternoon is put on my emu lotion and stare at the wall. She left my car in Oklahoma at a bus station. She'll never be found again; she's long gone. A nightmare that will forever plague me. I was a fly in the room, but I was caught in her web. Has she killed before? Who'll be next? That guy at the bar should consider himself lucky. Kelsey's own mom left her because she was scared of her.

I walk out and ask my hosts if they would be willing to give me a ride to Statesboro for some cash and that I would not need the last night.

"How about we call it even?" the man says. I gather my meager possessions, and we drive in silence. His wife stays home. My mind swirls with visions of the hotel room: blood, bags, bed, witnesses. I have no one to talk to. I would like to just spill my guts out right now and have a big emotional fit, but I'm now a new member of my dark family — the family that keeps emotional problems in to fester. A family that hides within themselves turmoil and secrets. This couple did tell me their names, but I can't remember them now. They're not important to my life or future, and being among others no longer means anything to me. I don't desire companionship any longer. I don't even explain why he's dropping me off at a police station. We wave goodbye.

This very elite agency has me fill out a form. I just put Mom's address down and hand it back. My car is driven around front, and this woman keeps standing beside me. The keys are in the ignition, and I leave before she notices anything like apprehension on my face. I am happy to see my car. After a few blocks, I pull into a donut shop and park under a tree. My entire life is here in this car, and my life is drastically different than it was three weeks ago. Will this altered path I am on now brighten soon? Or is this man in his car going to morph into a freak in a whole new way? Is the negative side of people all that I will see? *A plan, Paul. You need a plan. Savannah was your plan —remember? Just go.* A few days ago, people called me a hero, but that feeling is lost. I wish I felt the need to embrace my future, but I just want to crawl into a hole and hide. In about two years, I could wake up and try life again. A cocoon sounds perfect, and I could emerge with a whole new skin. I don't think I can handle much else going wrong.

Paul, time to get real. Sitting here in a parking lot will not help you out. I open the trunk. My things were ransacked, but I still have most of my clothes, sheets, towels, pans, and pictures. I have a little money in the bank. I have some cash from Mom, about $300 left. I should be thankful Kelsey didn't trash my car. My phone charger is still in the glove box, along with my sunscreen. I grab some donuts, put fifteen dollars worth of gas in the tank, and head to Savannah.

Signs are talking about the most haunted city in America, Leopold's ice cream, art galleries, antique shops, and Tybee Island. I drive in on Rt. 80 and turn south on Truman Parkway. Today is Wednesday, and the sun is shining. I see signs for a cemetery, but I would like to get settled first before I conjure up any spirits. I pass a golf course and some waterways and soon see a sign for Suburban Extended Stay Abercorn. There are rooms, but I can't get one without a credit card, which Kelsey took, and I am not calling Mom. I may have to find another Airbnb to stay in. This driving in the hot sun is making me tired. I head back north and see a sign for a hospital. I do know there are sometimes a lot of empty rooms, and I could make myself look like a patient. I laugh at the thought of hiding in rooms again, but it's not really funny. The thought of pretending to be a patient does amuse me. I pull up and realize this place is for the mentally challenged and disabled. Even better.

I laugh at myself again, because it's like I've found my island, after all. This might be right where I need to be; there might even be jobs here. I park in the visitor's lot and walk in; I see a man sitting in a chair to greet people. He tries to say "Hello," but it doesn't come out that way. He has a tray in front of him, like a big high chair. Is that a bib?

"Can you tell me where the office is?" He points down a hallway. I head in that direction and soon see a door labeled Human Resources. No use being shy. There is nothing to lose, and I will just let my dark side talk. There's a woman behind a desk. The little sign says her name is Myra Jackson. She smiles when I enter, an older lady with thin brown hair and big flowers on her shirt. She stammers a little when she really sees me.

"Hello, sir. Can I help you?"

"Hello, Myra. My name is Paul, and I'd like to ask if you have any jobs open."

"Well, yes, we do. Do you have a résumé?"

"No, but I just finished working at a hotel in Myrtle Beach for more than two years in their kitchen. I can give you their number if you want to call them for a reference."

"Okay. What did you do in the kitchen?"

"I washed the dishes," I say, hoping she won't even ask for the phone number. "I am very good at it — and fast. I would like to work full-time or possibly more, and I need to have temporary housing here for a while. I am looking to possibly live in the area, but I don't have a place yet. Just give me one day of work to show you." I will just tell them what I want. *Get what you want, Paul.*

"Paul, let me get my supervisor. Just a moment." I sit down to wait. Myra doesn't ask about my face or stare at me with eyes that can't look away. I like her. I'm left waiting for several minutes, looking at pictures framed that were done by what looks like kids, but probably not. Someone named Tyler did most of them. Not bad. They are all different animals with food hanging out of their mouths: turtle with leaves, horse with carrots, dog with bone, bear with berries on a twig, and a beetle holding what must be dung. Myra comes out with another woman, who walks over to shake my hand.

"Hello, my name is Jeanie. You're looking for employment and possibly a place to stay for a while?" She also smiles at me. Jeanie is short and wide and has a friendly face.

"Yes. Just give me a chance."

"Well, I am sure you realize we can't just hire someone off the streets to start working here and live here without the proper paperwork and background check. There is a process we must go through." Here goes nothing.

"Jeanie, do you remember the recent story of a fire in Reidsville at the state park and the kid who went in to save a woman after the cabin was set on fire?"

"Yes," she says.

"Well, that was me. I was nearly killed, and my wallet was stolen. I need a new place to start with a new job. I don't hang out with criminals or cause any problems. Look at me. I can't work just anywhere; these scars have plagued me my whole life.

Give me a chance to show you my job skills. If I leave here, I don't know where I will go next." She is absorbing what I said.

"Okay, let me give you a little tour, and I can ask you a few more questions." I follow her out. "We require a high school diploma and a photo ID. We will have to do a background check to work here, but if you are just in the kitchen and not involved with the patients in any way, we can probably work something out. I will need a couple of references though, Paul."

"I will be getting a new license for this state. The background check will not be a problem, and I can give you references — from policemen, even." We enter the kitchen. There are three women preparing the next feast and another woman doing the dishes. There is a dish tank similar to the one I was using but looks much older. There is food all over the floor, and dishes are piled up. The drains look clogged, and the woman is a sweaty mess. Yikes, I was right! Just give me one day.

"You are also required to take a drug test." She seems embarrassed for me to see the kitchen. Good.

"Let's do it right now, Jeanie. I want to get to work tomorrow, if possible." *Just tell them what you want; this philosophy is working out.*

"Okay, we can head to the nurse's station, and you can give us a sample."

"Are there rooms available?"

"Not many people actually live here — it's mostly outpatient. We do have some exceptions, and two staff members work each night." I urinate in a cup and give it back to the nurse. She smiles; everyone here seems nice.

"My drug test will come out clean, I'll have my license made this week, and my mom can fax my diploma from Michigan to you. How about you take twenty-five dollars per day out of my check to live here for a while, and I'll give you fifty hours per week. You obviously need it. The staff will love me, and I won't cause any trouble." She looks at me and agrees to give me a trial. Jeanie walks me to a back hallway.

"I would like to keep you a little further out of the way from the clients," she explains. "This will give you more privacy, also." Perfect. "These two rooms are used for storage, so pick one, and move the stuff into the other. The sheets and supplies are down the far hallway on the other side. The restroom is right there, but the showers are down the other hallway, also."

"Thank you so much."

"I will give you a chance, Paul, and we could use the help."

My drug screen comes out fine. She says I can start at 7:00 a.m. Wow, that totally worked. I just told them what I wanted. Some of the people here are still in the dining area. I saw some people being fed and some people covered in food. The rest of the folks are watching TV in the open lobby area. Some housing show is on, and it must be funny. I head back down to the storage rooms and choose the room that has a bed with less stuff heaped on it. I move boxes, plastic toilets, a lifting apparatus on wheels, walkers, and soft foamy cushions to the other room. I roll around a plastic cart and small metal trays on wheels. Now I am down to a bare bed and a closet. I walk up the far hallway and find the bedding, along with the toothbrushes, paste, combs, mouthwash, deodorant, dressing supplies, and women's things. I grab sheets and blankets, return to my room, and make up the bed. I go out to my car and grab some clothes, along with my nonskid shoes and work wear, which fit into the closet. I don't care about the dusty floor or the dirty mirror. I use the bathroom down the hall. I collapse into the bed exhausted and very pleased with myself. I should call Mom, but I will tomorrow after work.

A ROUND FIVE O'CLOCK, I smell something like beef and potatoes, and my stomach quickly wakes up. When I walk into the dining area, some people look my way for a moment, but then they are back to their routines. No silent stares. Most of the people here look odd, and I find myself staring at them. The ones with the severe disabilities are being fed, and other people are sitting around in the lobby. There are a few people going through a line, which is where I head to.

I sit down at an empty table and look at my cubed steak, mashed potatoes, and peas. I hope this is free; I doubt they have cheeseburger pizza here. Another man, probably in his thirties, brings his tray over to sit with me. He has a hard time walking and holding his tray at the same time. He moves very cautiously in his Velcro tennis shoes and sweatpants. One side of his face is droopy, and he drags his leg some on that side, but he finally manages. He starts eating and glances up at me while I glance occasionally up at him. Food falls out of his mouth once, but he doesn't seem to notice. He makes a little coughing sound while eating. Neither of us talk until we are done eating, and he starts.

"Whad wrong wich your face?" he asks me with a strange mouth movement.

"What's wrong with your face?" I return. He smiles.

"I had a sdoke lad year." He doesn't talk real clear, but I can understand him. "I had to relearn how do walk and dalk."

"I was burned when I was young."

"How wer ya durned?"

"I pulled a pot of chili onto myself from the stove."

"Why are ya dere?" he asks next.

"I needed a job. What's your name?"

"Miles Drumm, wid do mm's. I didn't dink ya wer dumb. Ya wer deeding yourseld."

"I'm Paul Duram. Do you live here?"

"During da weed. My dad gets me on da weedend. He has to word a lod, and I can'd be led alone. I fall somedimes. Hopefully, soon I'll be good enough to day at home."

Miles reaches out slowly and touches the top of my hand with his left hand. Then a lady comes over and offers to take our trays.

"Hi, there. I'm Teresa. I see you've met Miles. You must be the new dishwasher. I did hear that story about the fire at the cabins. Did that lady you saved do okay?" She talks real loud, and her hair is a bright pink color. She must be a little older than me, I'll guess.

"No, she died from the smoke later on," I answer.

"Oh, god. I'm sorry. I've been to those cabins before. Well, I'll see you tomorrow. I just work in the evening around here. Most people are just here for outpatient therapy, while the rest are here all day or live here. They are picked up after dinner by family and brought back in the morning while the family works."

"I see."

"See you tomorrow then." She takes our trays and heads to the back room. It's like she didn't even notice what I looked like sitting here. I don't know if she is a dishwasher or not.

Miles talks again. "She dalks a lot, but everyone is dice dere."

"I'm going to go now. See you later on, then," I say in case he is wanting to hang out all evening.

"Dye." He says. I get up and walk out to my car, and it is much cooler out. This place is strange to me; people actually walk right up and talk to me. I take some deep breaths and remind myself life is not as I perceived it — it's almost fictional now. I hear a distant noise, like an insect; maybe it's a cicada or something like that. The trees here are different too. There is a blue tint to them. *Paul, just breathe. So the trees and bugs are a little different, and people are talking to you. Remember what all you have been through lately. You can do this, and you are not going to hide anymore.*

Miles seems nice. Maybe I should have stayed and talked to him more, but I am not ready for long conversations with someone who is hard to understand. I remember having some long conversations with Kelsey. She was so easy to talk to. Was that all a part of her charm? Miles is probably safe to talk to, and I could use a new friend. It feels stupid to stand in the parking lot. I would go back to my room, but I have no TV or anything. Back in my old life, I would have gone home and put in one of my videos. *That life is gone; you're in Savannah now.* Bonnie wanted to just hang around the downtown area and watch people. I imagine doing that. I need to dig out my hat.

It has been such a long time since I've seen my sister. I suppose she would never come to Savannah to visit me, knowing it's full of ghosts — "the most haunted place in America." I will be on my own trying to conjure my paranormal self, if I can. I might not have the ability, like Mom. On my first day off, I will go back to that cemetery I passed and summon up some visions. Maybe I should call Tammy and ask for some advice on how to do that, but I'm sure the first conversation we have about her ability should not be over the phone. When I get time off, I'll go home, and we'll have our first heart-to-heart. Guilt over not knowing about her life and struggles overcomes me. It's like I wasn't even part of my own family. Almost like an outcast in my house, just like I am to the outside world. *Nobody tell Paul what's going on.* Now I wonder if my grandparents know about the visions.

I walk back inside and straight back to my room. Lights kept off, lying on the plastic-lined bed, and now thinking about her. Where is she? Is she sitting at a bar scamming for her next victim with her seductive talk? Someone she can manipulate into taking care of her and play her little games with? Maybe she is taking a bike ride all by herself so she can be with her thoughts. "Poor, poor me. I have no family, because my mom died of cancer and my uncle abused me and my boyfriend tried to kill me." I picture her lying in the dark like I am now, feeling sorry for …

Bang, Bang, Bang! Then a pause and two more loud *bangs*. I jump up, terrified. What was that, a gun? I freeze, waiting for more noise, quiet. I picture Kelsey finding me here and wanting to finish me off. I instinctively get under the bed and move to the top of the bed for some reason. I can hardly breathe, waiting for another *bang* to happen. A door bangs, and it's quiet again. I am breathing in all of the dustballs. Kelsey needs to get rid of the witness — me, the witness to her latest crime spree. I sense there are dead bugs all under me. Now I can see the dead worm bodies under my bed. Now I am under Dad's bed, and there are no dead worms here, but I just heard the loud banging. It surprised me, the banging. Then Dad yells to Tammy downstairs.

"He's coming down, he's coming down!" I thought they were just playing a game, like hide-and-seek. I wanted Dad to play with me, but I was too afraid to ask him. He never seemed to want to play with me or look at me. He was banging on the walls again. I stayed under the bed, so he wouldn't get mad at me for messing up their game. Then he yells again, "It's both of them!" It did sound like an intense game. Dad was scared. *It wasn't a game, Paul. You know that now.* Then I hear something, almost like laughter or cheering, from a distance. I slide out from under and listen while crouched on the far side of the room, feeling like an idiot, because I just heard more cheering.

I slowly make my way up the hallway to the TV room. Once in the light, I see all of the dust and pieces of dead bugs stuck to my clothes, which I brush off. Once close enough to see, there are several people watching *Jeopardy*.

"What was the banging sound?" I ask anyone who will answer me.

"Oh, sorry," Teresa says from behind me. "That was Travis. See, over there — with the pans? He announces every night when it is time for *Jeopardy* by banging the pans together. It's hard for him not to keep banging, but he knows he is only allowed to do that at the beginning of the show. He just likes to hold his pans." I look at Travis. He must be around my mom's age, with bib overalls on. He obviously gets very excited watching this show, and nobody sits near him.

"Is there anything else very loud that happens around here I should know about?" I ask her.

"Well, like I said, I'm here only in the evening, so there might be," she answers with a smile and walks on. I watch Travis for a little longer. He's like a big kid. I decide to take another look at the kitchen. When I see the dish room, there are bins full and piles of dirty dishes. I see one woman cleaning up the kitchen, putting food away; the floor is a mess. There's another woman cleaning up the floor around the tables. Nobody is even doing the dishes yet. Well, I'm not doing anything else, and Travis has got me wide awake. I go back to my room and put on my gear and get to work. My mind needs something else to do now.

After a surprisingly good night's sleep, I'm back in the kitchen at 7:00 a.m. There is nothing to do right away, because it is spotless from last night, when I unclogged the drain, cleaned the floor, and easily found where the clean dishes go. I even tightened some loose parts on the tank and scraped off some corrosion inside with the wire brush from the cleaning closet. The walls had a bit of grease buildup, but not now. The morning employees filter in, looking at the room with wide eyes.

"Normally, we have to finish cleaning the dishes from last night," one says. "I bet you did that, right?"

"Yep, I couldn't help myself, and I had nothing better to do."

"Hi, I'm Megan. I guess you won't have anything to do for a while now. LuAnn is in charge of the kitchen if you need something. Do you need some gloves?"

"No, I'm good," I answer. "Thanks." She walks out. Megan is cute, with short dark hair. Young, like Teresa, but doesn't talk as much or have pink hair. Around 8:00 a.m., the dishes start coming in, and I have them washed and put away before the big pans show up. I keep the water running on hot to clear out the drain even more and prewash the pans. I wonder if some of these are Travis's pans, or does he keep his own? I chuckle. An older lady walks in, who I'm guessing is LuAnn.

"You do a great job ... Paul, is it?"

"Yes, thank you."

"When you are done in here, if you wouldn't mind helping with the dining-room floors, that would be great."

"Sure."

When all of the crazies are gone, Megan and I sweep and clean the floors. Then I am told to come back at noon. I decide I better return Mom's calls now.

A FTER THREE DAYS OF working, I'm given a day off. I have
eaten with Miles two more times, and Travis bangs away
at the same time each evening. I cleaned the floors in my room,
and Jeanie has let me borrow an old computer to play some
games on. They are pleased with my work, of course. Megan
is fun; it is a little bit like having Taylor again. She has worked
here for almost two years while she goes to school during the
evening to become a chef. She asked me yesterday how I got
burned and could not believe I got burned over most of my
body a second time. We both talked about our families. I told
her minor details about mine. Mom told me that Tammy and
Johnny are getting married this Christmas — the whole family will be together and for me to make sure I get time off to
finally come. Mom wondered if they found out where Kelsey
was, but I haven't received any news. Mom and Megan both

asked how I liked Savannah, but I have not explored it yet. Not till today, my day off.

I drive north, back up Harry Truman Parkway, to the Bonaventure Cemetery. After parking a block away, I slowly walk toward it. I'm wearing one of my old baseball caps and a long-sleeved shirt. There aren't many people around today. It's windy, and the trees are swaying. The long branches hang down all around, like arms. I walk along an iron fence before entering — an iron fence like at the Reidsville Cemetery. Is the iron fence supposed to keep spirits in or out? Is that symbolic somehow? I enter, and the headstones cause a sharp knot in my stomach. Carved statues of girls, tall headstones, short ones, moss-covered, captured under the swaying trees; it all speaks through the separation of entities. *You're in our world now. You came in, so don't get mad if you don't like it. It was your choice.* The headstones are like soldiers marching, at "Parade Rest" or a band waiting, in unison, for the director (or drill sergeant) to tell them when to move again. The stillness of the stones is such a contrast to the swaying of the trees. It entices me to watch the show that's about to start.

I find a little bench toward the back. There is more moss growing along surfaces, like another world is taking over. I wonder if worms like moss. There is a chill in the air under the shade of the wavy, droopy arms. Wow, I can see why this is the "city of spirits"; it is creepy and beautiful. It is another world — death's world. Okay, if I am going to channel anything, this would be the place. I relax and take some deep breaths. I slowly look around — very slowly — between the stones and beside each tree, scanning for a vision. I can smell the musk, and I can hear the cicadas hissing. The insects seem bigger here, which adds to the creepy feeling. The trees are trying to hide what goes on here, to distract from the death with their beauty. Do I actually hear woodpeckers in the distance? Not sure, but I see nothing. No ghosts or spirits or train engineers. I close my eyes to see if anything talks to me ... and nothing. After sitting here nearly an hour, it seems futile.

Megan told me to see River Street and take a drive to the beach. I leave the cemetery, slowly walking out and looking back twice — nothing. That was disappointing. I find River Street and finally find a place to park. I walk around and see the river and restaurants, but I feel isolated again. For a short time, I had companions. People were with me, and we talked together, but that was short-lived. Kelsey's face enters my mind, and I hate her. I feel so ignorant about all the stuff going on around me, and I was clueless. Clueless about my family and clueless about who I thought were my friends. I want to get away from people and drive.

I now see the Tybee Island sign. I drive on Islands Expressway, and I'm blown away by all the waterways and enormous houses. The closer I get, the houses get even bigger. I don't think I'll find any trailer parks around here. Then it hits me — trailer park. I need to pull over, but I want to get to the beach first; I'm almost there. I see the ocean ahead. I randomly pull over and walk toward the water, with the hot sun shining and people milling about. I pull out my phone and scan my pictures. There is the secret picture I took of my trailer while Kelsey and I were waiting for Bonnie to get her things together. Kelsey was sitting between me and the trailer, and I snapped a picture without her knowing. There it is, and there she is. It is just her head, and she's looking a little to the side, but it is a clear shot of her. Oh, my God — I had a photo of Kelsey all along!

I want to scream at this beach and the water and the sky, make it all listen to me. Here's a picture. It's not from eight years ago, when she looked like a child in her high school picture, or a toddler picture her mom had in her wallet. It is her now — her hair, her jawline, her nose, and her eyes, those penetrating eyes that will lie with every word that comes out of that mouth. Maybe they can find her now. Maybe she is in a "Reidsville" somewhere. Maybe she's already working at another home-security company, finding her next smart little nerd. The police can post her face, but I suppose Kelsey Raymond will not be a top priority; she will just be on a list. She could be anywhere now.

I need a drink; I need water now. I drive to the nearest drive-through, ask for two large waters, find a spot in the shade to sit, and call Officer Kevin. I leave a message for him to call me back. After drinking both waters, I feel better, mentally and physically. I probably wasn't drinking enough now that I am working more, and the heat is stronger here. It will be October soon. This beach will clear out, but the water will just keep rushing in, over and over, the powerful tide, able to strike when needed. Ready to take you out with one big burst. Her own mom left her one night without a word. Her mom knew it was only a matter of time till her daughter would strike.

My phone is silent. I am ready to go back to my temporary home. I am not sure how long I will stay in my storage
room — or in Savannah — but for now, this is okay. Driving
back, I will my phone to ring. I arrive back to crazy-town and
walk in. Miles is on the phone.

"Do dozen, dure, come on ove," he says and then tries to
stand up from the TV-room couch.

"Where are you going?" I ask.

"Come on, I'll dow ya." I follow him out a back door to a
small greenhouse made with plastic; he opens the door and
walks in. I see bags of dirt and big plastic bins stacked up on
racks. There are air holes in all of them.

"What is this? Is it all yours?"

"Yea, I drow worms and dell em."

I'm speechless. Worms, my childhood fetish. He opens
the large container on the table and fills a cup from his plain-
dirt bag; then he reaches in and starts pulling out handfuls of
big, plump worms, my favorite kind. There must be hundreds
of them or even thousands of them in here. He slowly counts
them out to twenty-four and puts the lid on.

"May I touch?" I ask with a big smile on my face — my
hands are nearly in the dirt already. He nods. The dirt seems
cool and loose and smells a little funny. I pull out two big
worms and hold them in my hands. They are so plump and
strong. I feel along the ridges but can't really feel the ridges.
Miles watches me as I become lost in my own little world.

"I dess you dike worms?" I nod and continue to hold my
two little friends. They can move faster than what I remember,
unless these are special worms I have never seen. They leave a

~ 174 ~

dense mucus trail on my hands. Then, my phone starts ringing, so I put them back and wipe my hands off on my pants.

"Excuse me," I say to Miles. I walk back into the building for some privacy; it's Officer Kevin calling me back.

"Hello. This is Kevin Brown." I guess he doesn't have me on caller ID like Corbin does.

"Hi, Officer Kevin. This is Paul Duram." There is a slight pause.

"Oh yeah, Paul. How are you? What's up?"

"Well, I'm a little embarrassed to tell you this now, but I found a picture of Kelsey on my phone that I didn't remember I had."

"Really? Well, that's great. Can you send it to me now on a text? I'll see what we can do with it."

"Yes. Do you think it will help?"

"Well, if she does anything again, it will surely help, but until then, it'll be hard to track her down. I'll put it into the NCIC system as a person to be on the lookout for, but I'm afraid that that's a big system. It's a start, though."

"Okay. Well, I'll send it now, and let me know if … well if … anything … happens."

"Of course, Paul. I look forward to getting it. We won't post her picture to the public quite yet so that she doesn't change her appearance. Having her picture might be all we need. Bye for now." Picture sent. The thought of waiting till she does something else is harsh. This is disheartening. I guess you've got to kill more than one or two people to be on a higher-priority list. I contemplate having her picture all along. *Stupid.*

I walk back outside, and Miles is talking to a guy; then the guy leaves with his worms. Miles puts cash in his pocket.

"When did you start doing this?"

"Afder my droke, I dove to fich, and id is hard dor me to do now."

"So you raise worms for others to fish?"

"I get, I get do ear fiching dories dis way. My dad dake me omedime."

"I have never been fishing," I say.

Miles drops his chin and turns to look at me in shock.

"I haven't."

He shakes his head.

The next morning, I start at 7:00 a.m., and there are dirty dishes, pans, glasses, and those stupid little plastic containers waiting for me from last night. I think about that picture and if it will do any good. Last night, I googled how many states have a "Reedsville" in them. I couldn't find an answer without looking at each state. She may have decided to change her game also, since I noticed it and mentioned it to her. Does she even know if I'm still alive?

I notice later that my sister had called me. I call her back after the lunch mess.

"Paul, I need to tell you something, and I want you to listen closely."

"Okay." She has never been one for small talk. "I hear you're getting married this …"

"Paul! Listen to me. I am glad to hear you are doing okay and all, but I have to get a message to you."

A message — this is very strange. She has my attention now. "Wasn't Bonnie the name of the lady who was your neighbor who died in the fire?"

"Yeah." My heart skips a beat.

"Well, she wants me to tell you something. She tried to tell you the other day in the cemetery, but you didn't pick up on her."

"Oh, my God, Tammy. She's talking to *you?*"

"Um … yes … I know this might sound strange to you, but she wants me to tell you 'Thank you' and that she hopes you like it in Savannah. But the most important thing is that she keeps saying, 'Kelsey, Wisconsin, Kelsey, Wisconsin.' That's what she wants me to tell you. Hopefully, now she'll quit repeating it."

"That's where Kelsey is — Wisconsin." I sink down to the floor.

I T IS GETTING CLOSE TO Halloween time. This town is outrageous. The décor and costumes are already in full swing
two weeks before it's even Halloween and it's how I would
imagine Mardi Gras. I feel like I could just accentuate my
normal look — and I would fit right in. Savannah is its own
little world. Bonnie was right about wanting to be here and
just watch life happen around you. I have now seen all of the
beautiful architecture. The famous buildings are outfitted for
the occasion: Mercer House, Eliza Thompson House, Comer
House, and Hamilton Turner House. I have seen the museums and been to the Moon River Brewing Company, which
is supposed to be haunted — but, nothing. The underground
tour was one of my favorites.

I now live on Myrtle Street — ironic. I rent a duplex with
a couple. It takes only about seven minutes to get to work
from here. My furniture is all used and came with the place.

I have inherited a cat that comes in and out the cat door. I have purchased a few new things: a straw cowboy hat to cover up a little more, some shoes, and a screwdriver set of multiple sizes. I also ride my new bike to work, and I feel stronger than ever. Sometimes between the morning and noon wash, I spend time in the cemetery to see if anything happens, but it remains quiet. I imagine Bonnie is there with me, still my neighbor, just in a different location. I have caught myself talking to her.

Mom is coming down next week to have some Halloween fun with me. She wants to see the museums and art galleries. Tammy said she will not be coming down. We had a little talk after she told me about Bonnie. I told her that I now realized she and Dad had the ability to see the dead, and I was sorry I wasn't really there for her. She cried and said she was sorry she didn't tell me; she thought that, if she told me, it might spread. My grandparents have all come to see me, but they spend more time sightseeing, which is fine. They like staying in my new place and sleeping on my bed while I sleep on my neighbor's front-porch swing.

Kelsey was caught recently. There is a Reidsville in Wisconsin, but there's more than one bar. The police staked out the four bars each night with an undercover officer. On the fourth night, an officer saw her dancing with some guy and arrested her on the spot; she looked just like the picture. She was at a bar called Spudz. They searched her belongings and found some of Bonnie's financial paperwork in her suitcase lining. They really don't need any more proof; she was on camera buying the gasoline with my car. Her trial is in January, and I will have to testify — no problem. The guy she was with thought she was an environmentalist. He is a descendant of the founders of Ocean Spray juice company.

Is there more peace in my life now that she's been caught? Yes. Life here has become even more exciting than beach life. Savannah doesn't care what anyone looks like as long as you respect the spirit. I think I'll stay here for a while.

Megan and I are good friends. I have considered asking her out on a date, but it doesn't feel right, because she stares at a new employee often whose name is Julia. Miles's aphasia is doing better, along with his walking. He has me sell his worms for him when he goes away for the weekends with his dad; I get to keep half of the profits.

Bonnie quit talking to Tammy long ago, so I wonder if she's still around. I asked my sister why she works at an antique store. Wouldn't there be lots of spirits with all of the old furniture? She said "No"; she thinks they don't like to compete with each other. Tammy explained that ghosts are solitary and that they make themselves known for unfinished business. If there is more than one spirit together, one will drive the other away. That's what was happening in our house when Dad took his life. Spirits were fighting each other for the house and involving Dad in their war. She said that Dad has told her to tell me he loved me and was never ashamed of me. It broke my heart to realize he knew my thoughts. I asked her if he still comes around, and she said that he doesn't. He must have said what he needed to say and moved on. I can picture the faraway look in his eyes, which wasn't revulsion toward me but a glare into worlds unknown. Tammy has that glare, too; she can see the entrance to that world, full of anything from peaceful train engineers to volatile entities.

I got invited to a party for Teresa. She is moving to New Mexico with her husband. Jeanie is having it at her house — my first friend party. Miles is coming, too, in my car. I will wear my new hat and my favorite old Michigan shirt. It will be this Sunday evening; we don't serve on Sunday evenings. We all went in together to buy her a gift certificate to some fancy store.

I am anxious to go home for the wedding. I am ready to face all of my family again. Yes, I am the guy who was under the bed and killed a man with a screwdriver. I will just tell everyone to check under their bed at night, because I'm getting that old feeling again. I laugh at myself. Apparently voyeurism is no joke, I have come to understand. I do notice the nice couple across the street from me, Brian and Bridget. I wonder what she smells like.

Tomorrow will be another new experience for me. Miles and his dad are taking me fishing. Someone else will have to hook the worm.

ABOUT THE AUTHOR

Kristi Downard is an avid fan of suspenseful fiction. After working as a nurse for thirty years, she decided she could tell a tale unlike any you have read. Kristi is currently working on a new book scheduled for release in 2021. She lives in Ohio with her family.

Made in the USA
Monee, IL
07 July 2020